About the Author

JANET AYLMER is an English author who enjoys reading historical romances set in the early 1800s. Her favorite writer is Georgette Heyer, whose stories feature the trials and tribulations of a lively heroine and a handsome hero living in the turbulent times when Jane Austen was writing her famous novels.

Julia
and the
Master of Morancourt

ALSO BY JANET AYLMER

FICTION

Darcy's Story

NONFICTION

*In the Footsteps of Jane Austen: Through Bath to
Lyncombe and Widcombe: A Walk Through History*

Julia

and the

Master of Morancourt

JANET AYLMER

HARPER

NEW YORK • LONDON • TORONTO • SYDNEY

HARPER

HarperCollins books may be purchased for educational, business, or sales promotional use. For information please write: Special Markets Department, HarperCollins Publishers, 10 East 53rd Street, New York, NY 10022.

FIRST EDITION

Designed by Joy O'Meara

Library of Congress Cataloging-in-Publication Data
Aylmer, Janet.
Julia and the master of Morancourt / Janet Aylmer.—1st ed.
p. cm.
ISBN 978-0-06-167295-8
1. Young women—England—Fiction. 2. Gentry—England—Fiction. 3. Derbyshire (England)—Fiction. 4. England—Social life and customs—19th century—Fiction. I. Title.
PR6101.Y46J86 2009
823'.92—dc22   2008051448

09 10 11 12 13 OV/RRD 10 9 8 7 6 5 4 3 2 1

This book is for
Joss and Stephanie
who know why Dorset is so special

Julia
and the
Master of Morancourt

ONE

The noise of the wheels of the old carriage rumbling along the uneven track almost drowned out the sound of the shoes tapping on the floor.

Almost, but not quite.

"Julia, why do you keep tapping your shoes?"

There was no answer. Her sister was intent on looking out of the window, at the rather grey day, at the bare green fields and the low stone walls that divided them into a green patchwork quilt. Beside her, on the worn leather seat, was the old tapestry bag containing their riding boots, waiting ready for the treat to come.

"Julia," persisted Sophie, "why are you tapping your shoes?"

Their father stirred from dozing on the seat opposite them and opened his eyes. "What did you say, Sophie?"

"Why is Julia tapping her feet, Papa?"

Lewis Maitland looked down at the worn old red shoes.

She had insisted on wearing them. Perhaps they were familiar, comforting, in a situation he knew that Julia would have preferred to avoid. Her face seemed paler than usual, and she had drawn her hair back from her face this morning in a rather severe style, the golden-brown curls more disciplined than usual above her brown riding skirt and short yellow jacket.

But his eldest daughter had heard his voice and, ignoring

her sister, turned her head to look at him. He returned her quiet smile before Julia said, "If you keep being a nuisance, Sophie, Mr. Douglas may not allow you to ride any of his horses."

Her sister did not look in the least abashed at this remark, but decided that it might not be a good idea to ask the question again.

"Papa, are you warm enough?"

Julia leant across to tuck the rug around him more snugly. His greatcoat had several capes, but it worried her that he was feeling the cold so much nowadays, and he always refused to wear any gloves on his thin hands.

Her father reflected, not for the first time, how very different the two sisters were. His eldest daughter had inherited her mother's grey eyes, and her determination, certainly, but in most other respects—her calmer personality, her sympathy for other people, her love of books, and her practical and independent mind—she was quite unlike Olivia.

Sophie, on the other hand, was quite irrepressible, ran at everything in life at full tilt, and could be very thoughtless about the needs of others. Harriet, the youngest, was a mixture of the two. But she was almost sixteen now, and it might be that she had changed during her last few months away at school.

Sophie fidgeted on her seat, and Julia said, "I suppose that what you really want to know is how long it will be before we get there?"

"Well, why shouldn't I? We seem to have been sitting on these uncomfortable seats for ages. Papa, you promised me that the journey would take no more than thirty minutes!"

"It is only twenty minutes since we left home, Sophie."

She looked rebellious, and twisted her hair in her fingers beneath her chip straw hat.

Their father, anxious to preserve a precarious peace, changed the subject.

"Harry Douglas has several good horses, and he has been very kind in saying that you may ride one, Sophie. Aren't you looking forward to that?"

"Oh, yes, of course I am, Papa. But I don't like sitting in the carriage for so long, and it keeps making that really horrible squeaking noise. I hate it!"

Her father turned the conversation back to the ride that she and Julia had been promised later in the afternoon.

"You will see that the stables were built at the same time as the mansion, but the farm buildings are a more recent addition. I believe that they have been constructed by Harry Douglas since his wife died, when young Jack decided that he was more interested in farming, like his grandfather, than in any other occupation."

Sophie was not interested in buildings—what she wanted was to go out straight away on one of the horses housed in the stables. "Does he ride often?"

"Mr. Douglas?"

"No, his son Jack—he is the person Julia is really going to see, isn't he?"

Her father looked at Julia, but her head was turned away from him, so he looked back again at Sophie.

He did not answer her directly. "Most people who live on a large estate would need to ride some of the time, but I don't imagine that Harry Douglas will want to go out today, so I will probably stay in the house with him whilst you and Julia ride with Jack, and maybe his brother."

"Brother?"

"Yes, there is a younger brother, just back from the war with Napoléon."

"What's his name?" said Sophie.

"Christopher—the family call him Kit."

Julia was getting bored with her younger sister's conversation. She did not know anything about Kit, but she had already heard that Jack Douglas was very careless of his horses, and a daredevil rider. That was one of the matters that she had decided to put out of her mind when her father had pressed her to agree to the visit. At least Jack should get on well with Sophie, for she was fearless in the saddle, as impetuous as she was in her conversation.

Julia turned to look again out of the carriage window. Most of Derbyshire was a mixture of valleys and steep hills, but this locality seemed to be an endless flat panorama of fields and walls. However, it was at last giving way to gently rounded slopes and groups of trees close to the road. Perhaps they had not got too much further to go now, and certainly Sophie would probably lose her temper if she had to sit still very much longer.

Soon after, the noise of the wheels on the track began to change from a loud rumble to a more gentle and even sound. As they rounded a bend, tall brownish stone pillars came into view with a lodge in the same local stone on each side, the two houses being linked by an archway over a handsome pair of iron gates. The carriage slowed, then paused, and a man came forward from one of the lodges to let them through.

"Papa, Papa, we're there at last!"

"Not quite, Sophie. You'll see in a while."

Julia soon realised that her father was right, as it took fully another ten minutes for them to reach the house. She could see that Sophie was very impressed by the size of the park, for their father had said little about the Norton Place estate beyond hinting that the family was financially very secure.

Here, the gravelled drive was bordered on each side by low

well-kept wooden fences to keep the sheep and deer from straying onto the track.

The only trees visible were in the further distance, on the lower slopes of the hills that formed a natural bowl surrounding the mansion. To one side, a stream widened into a lake close to the house, and then tumbled down a waterfall and away along the valley. On the other, the extensive block of stables built at right angles to the main building enclosed a courtyard where the carriage was brought to a halt at the foot of a long flight of stone steps.

Julia had not expected to be pleased by the appearance of the mansion, but found herself liking the gracious symmetry of the main facade and the tall windows, and the simple but elegant formal garden on each side.

An elderly groom came forward and opened the carriage door so that they could alight. Sophie tumbled down onto the forecourt, and the groom came forward to help Julia and their father descend at a more sedate pace.

"Welcome, welcome, Lewis!" The booming voice came from a stout red-faced gentleman standing between the stone pillars at the top of the wide stone steps by the main doors. He came down the steps to greet them.

"Thank you, Harry. May I introduce my daughters, Julia Maitland—and not forgetting Sophie?" Both the young ladies curtsied to their host.

"Indeed, you are both very welcome. I wish that we had such fine young ladies living in this house."

Julia found his rather effusive style of speaking rather disconcerting, but Sophie was delighted. After all, she was eighteen years old now, but was always chafing at her more junior status in the family. Only the fact that Harriet was two years younger made her feel like the grown-up young lady she felt she had now become.

"Do you want the bag with you, Miss?"

They both turned, and the groom gestured towards the tapestry bag still resting on the seat of the carriage. Before Julia could reply, Sophie pushed forward and took it. Clutching the handle, Sophie started to walk up the steps.

"Sophie!" She stopped as Julia checked her. "Wait for Mr. Douglas to conduct us."

Their host laughed. "I like to see a young lady with spirit." And to the coachman he said, "Please take the carriage round to the stables."

Then Mr. Douglas took their father's arm and they walked up the steps with the two sisters following behind.

As she passed through the front door, the butler took the tapestry bag from Sophie and put it on a chair with a velvet seat. She was about to protest but thought better of it when she saw Julia's expression.

Sensing her urgency, Mr. Douglas said, "I don't know where Jack is, but he can't be far away. Reuben, go and tell him that Miss Maitland and Miss Sophie have arrived. He's probably somewhere in the farm buildings."

The groom hurried away, and their father followed Harry Douglas through the doorway.

Inside, a handsome wooden staircase with a graceful balustrade curved away towards the rear of the hall and then split into two parts to reach the first floor. Beyond stone pillars on each side, panelled doors could be seen leading to several spacious reception rooms, and straight ahead the park outside was visible through several tall windows. Large paintings hung on the walls above more velvet chairs, and a large Turkish carpet occupied the centre of the floor. Mama would be impressed by all this, Julia thought.

The soles of her shoes echoed on the wooden floor as they were led along a wide corridor to the left, passing a large formal dining room, and they were about to enter the main salon at the end when Julia caught sight of a library on the right side of the corridor. Mr. Douglas paused and spoke to someone within.

"Kit, here are Lewis Maitland and his two daughters." And he led the way into the room. The library was large and lined with tall bookshelves on every side, which were full of volumes from floor to ceiling.

Sitting at a table on the far side of the room was a young man with dark hair who looked up as they came in. He laid down his pen on a list that he had been writing and, rising from his seat, came forward to meet them, limping slightly. His clear green eyes met Julia's grey ones as their host made the introductions.

"Mr. Lewis Maitland, Miss Maitland, Miss Sophie, this is my son Kit Douglas," and to his son, he continued, "Miss Maitland, I am told, is very fond of books."

Turning to Julia, he added, "Is that not so?"

"Yes, sir—what a well-stocked library! Perhaps I might be allowed to have a look at some of the books later on? It's true, I am fond of reading."

"But of course," said Mr. Douglas, looking at his son who, after a slight pause, said, "Miss Maitland, would you like to look at the list of our latest acquisitions now?"

"Oh, I should love to do that. Would you excuse me, Mr. Douglas, for a short while?"

"But of course, my dear. I rarely look at a book, being much more of a practical man myself. The library here was created by my wife, who brought some of the books from her family's home. And our son Kit here has continued her interest."

Behind them, Sophie fidgeted at the delay. Noticing this, her host said to Julia, "Lewis and I will take your sister into the drawing room for some light refreshments before you both go riding."

And he led his other guests out through the panelled double doors towards the corridor, leaving Julia with Kit Douglas.

"Miss Maitland, if you will come to the table, you can look at my list of books and choose some volumes to see."

Julia crossed the room and sat down on a chair that he had pulled forward next to him. There were several sheets of paper filled with neat writing, which he explained listed the titles and authors of a pile of books on the far side of the table.

"These are some volumes that I purchased on the Continent, before I came home. Which ones will you choose?"

Kit Douglas handed the sheets to her and she looked through them quickly. Then she pointed at three books on the list.

"You have unusual tastes in literature, Miss Maitland."

She looked at him rather warily, and then caught a hint of humour in his expression, so she said, "My father has always encouraged me to read widely. You consider that inappropriate for a young lady?"

This time he smiled quite broadly. "If I had any sisters, Miss Maitland, I'm sure that they should have access to the same range of volumes as I do."

He chose the books that she had indicated from the pile and handed them to her. "I purchased two of these whilst I was in Spain, for my regiment was quartered in an old town where there was a very interesting bookshop."

"Oh, have you been to the Peninsula? Did you meet my brother David there?"

"No, I did not have that pleasure. My father said that he was in the same regiment as the Brandon brothers."

His manner seemed to her to be rather serious, but that was more to Julia's liking than the brasher style of many young men.

"You, too, like books very much? Are these all from the Continent?"

"Yes, all those here on the side table—but we have many others on the shelves, as you can see."

Julia looked quickly through two of the books, conscious of being scrutinised with a clear gaze. When she came to the last volume, the smallest one, she opened it carefully, and then cried out with delight. For it was a Book of Hours, bound in pale brown leather and beautifully illustrated with pictures in many colours highlighted with gold leaf, and with the text written in Latin on cream-colored calfskin.

"So you like *La Passerelle*?" he said.

"Oh yes, very much. Is that the French title?"

He took the book and opened it towards the end of the volume. "Not the title—perhaps you would call it a nickname. If you look at this picture, can you see that there is a bridge, reaching across to the next world? See how the artist has coloured the details of the bridge very carefully, using extra detail in gold leaf as it reaches towards heaven?"

"Oh, of course—bridge, gangway—that is *la passerelle* in French!"

"Yes, exactly right. I came across the book by chance, and I had to buy it."

She smiled at him. "I can quite understand why."

He hesitated, and then said, "I purchased it as a gift, but I was unable to deliver the book to the person for whom it was intended."

There was something in his manner that prevented her from asking more. In any case, it was none of her business.

He coughed politely, and Julia remembered where she was.

"Perhaps we should join the others in the salon now, Miss Maitland. Otherwise, you may not have time for any refreshments before our ride. I hope that you will allow me to accompany you and your sister?"

She inclined her head without speaking, and followed him along the corridor to where her father was sitting with Mr. Douglas and Sophie in the salon, eating some small cakes with a glass of cordial.

"Please excuse the delay, Mr. Douglas, it was entirely my fault," said Julia, as she sat down to join them.

"Not at all, my dear, I am pleased that you enjoyed yourself," said her host.

Before they could make any more conversation, there was a commotion at the other end of the corridor, and a thick-set young man of middle height, wearing riding boots and carrying a whip in his hand, came rushing into the room, followed by the groom.

He came up to Sophie, who was sitting next to Mr. Douglas, and said, "I'm here now, Father. Are you Miss Maitland? I hope that you are ready?"

"Jack!" exclaimed his father, but Sophie, unabashed, said, "No, I am Sophie Maitland. That is my elder sister, Julia, over there, with your brother."

Harry Douglas interrupted them. "Here you are at last, Jack! Introduce yourself properly to our guests, for goodness' sake. You should have been at the front door some twenty minutes ago to greet them."

Julia was surprised at his impatience, for she had persuaded herself in advance of the visit that Jack, as the elder son, would be his father's favourite. But the tone of voice Harry Douglas had just employed was very much more demanding than that he had used a few minutes earlier to his younger son.

Jack Douglas had his father's broad frame and red face, his loud voice and his rather rough way of speaking. His style of dress was untidy, his fair hair unruly, and his hands large. By comparison, his younger brother was nearly a head taller, and his clothes, though not in the very latest fashion, were neat and well kept, his complexion tanned by the sun, and his wavy dark hair carefully combed.

Sophie was not going to be deterred much longer from her purpose. "Papa, Papa, may I go and put on my boots now— please let me—then we can go riding? Please!"

Sensing the inevitable, her father smiled wearily at Julia, and he and Sophie left the room with Jack Douglas. His brother, Kit, excused himself and went after them with the groom, leaving Julia in the library with his father.

Before she could follow, Mr. Douglas said in a quieter voice, "Miss Maitland? Your father, Lewis, how is he? I had heard that his heart had been troubling him again. He looks rather worn. That concerns me very much."

"It's true that he is still not well, sir, and he worries so about the future for all of us, now that the estate will go to our cousin after him."

Julia might have hesitated, but his kind manner encouraged her to continue. "It is very kind of you to try to help by introducing me to Jack, though it seems that I may need to compete with Sophie for his attention!"

"Jack is twenty-seven years old now but, unless he acquires

more gentlemanly manners, he may never be what I had hoped. My sons are very different and it is Kit who takes after my late wife. She was always quietly considerate of others."

As he spoke, he looked up at the portrait hanging on the wall of a tall dark-haired woman who bore a strong resemblance to his younger son.

"As the owner of Norton Place, I have a local living here where I control the choice of the new curate, but Kit was never interested in entering the church, so I encouraged him to join the regiment, and he did very well. I had purchased him a commission in the Hussars, and then he was off to Spain. But all too soon he was wounded in an engagement with the French and, before he came home, my wife died suddenly."

Mr. Douglas paused and blew his nose loudly on a large spotted handkerchief.

"Your family's loss in the next battle was much greater than ours, but both young men were unlucky, for in each case the army had won a great victory—celebrated, of course, by those officers and men who survived."

"You are right, sir, for Dominic Brandon returned with the sad news of my brother's death in the war with Napoléon."

"Yes. But for your father, for that to be followed so soon by his losses because of the bank failing in Derby, it was such bad timing." And he patted her shoulder in a fatherly way.

It is very odd, Julia thought. She had been so prepared to be wary of this man, and yet she now found that they were quite in sympathy with each other. Perhaps the common bond was her father and their affection for him, or maybe it was that she just felt confident that Harry Douglas was not pretentious but genuine, and keen to act in her best interests.

A quiet voice from the doorway intervened. Kit Douglas had returned and was standing watching them both.

"Father, we must go now to catch up with Jack and Miss Sophie, or they will leave on the ride without us. I fear that Jack might lead Miss Maitland's sister on a dangerous route without thinking of the consequences."

Turning towards Julia with a slow smile, he added, "Your sister seems to be a determined young lady."

"Perhaps you really mean headstrong?"

"I did not choose to put it that way, for fear of being rebuked."

"I must remember to be careful what words I use in your company, Mr. Douglas."

"I rather believe, Kit," said his father, laughing, "that you might have met your match at last in this young lady."

"Perhaps, sir," said his son, "but we really must go now before they leave for the ride." He added, "Your sister asked me to tell you, Miss Maitland, that she has taken the tapestry bag and will leave it in the carriage, but your own riding boots await you in the hall."

Escorted by Kit Douglas to the hall, Julia took off her red shoes, gave them to the butler, and laced up her boots.

By the time they had reached the stables, Jack Douglas and Sophie were already mounted. Her sister's pretty bay was just the right size for a girl of middle height and, to Julia's relief, did not seem to be too skittish. Jack had a fine chestnut stallion, which was already pawing the ground with impatience to be off.

The stable lad was holding the reins of two more horses, and Reuben helped Julia to mount and settle comfortably side saddle on a grey roan. Kit Douglas was soon astride his large stallion, and the four young people rode out of the stable yard. On their way, they passed the steps to the main entrance of the house, where Harry Douglas and Julia's father were standing by the front door to wave them on their way.

"I suggest that we take the route up the valley, Jack, and then once we have emerged from the trees, go along the ridge where there will be a pleasant view over the park. I am sure that the young ladies would enjoy seeing that panorama."

"I suppose that we could go that way, Kit," said his brother, "but it would be much more fun, once we reach the higher ground, if we take the longer route across the fields and down the valley on the far side. There are some good jumps over the low stone walls there."

Julia could see that his brother did not favour this idea, but Sophie exclaimed, "Oh, yes please, Mr. Douglas, I do enjoy jumping!"

Before either Julia or Jack's brother could protest, their companions set off at a fast trot up the slope, and only paused to wait for them once they had reached the very top of the hill. Julia rode behind with Kit Douglas at a more steady pace but, just as they were going to reach the others, Jack turned his mount to the left and Sophie followed him, cantering along and then out of sight over the ridge.

"You don't like that route, Mr. Douglas?"

"No, Miss Maitland. The walls are not as low as my brother suggests. Is your sister a safe rider in a tight situation? If not, she could come to grief. I suggest that we ride a little further this way, and then we shall have a good view of them as they reach the jump over the first wall."

They rode as Kit Douglas had suggested, and paused at a viewpoint overlooking the further valley. Quite soon, Jack and his companion came into view, and Julia could see that they were heading for a stout stone wall at the far side of a large field. Kit Douglas was right, the wall was quite high, and Sophie was riding a small mare. However, that did not deter her.

Julia held her breath and almost closed her eyes in concentration as the moment came for Sophie's mount to jump the wall.

"Oh, thank goodness," she said, "she's over safely."

"Yes—she did very well. But my brother did not. Look to the right, can you see—his mount refused and he was tangled in the reins as he fell."

"Oh, I do apologise. I had quite forgotten about your brother. Is he hurt?"

"Probably not, but he will not be pleased that your young sister has shown him up. Perhaps one day he will learn not to show off. My father will be delighted that your sister had such success compared to Jack!"

He turned in the saddle as he spoke and caught her surprised expression.

"I can see that you disapprove?"

"I would not speak of my father like that," said Julia slowly.

"But it's true. Am I being harsh? Perhaps so—Jack usually does what he wants to, whether it is sensible or not. He will not help our father manage the rest of the estate. I would love to do that, but I am not the elder son. That is one reason why I went off to make my career in Spain, as an officer in Wellington's army, but this wretched wound will probably prevent me from continuing that career—and anyway, now my father really wants me to stay in England."

Julia was still annoyed with him, but she tried not to show it.

"Why would your father be delighted that Jack fell?" said Julia.

"Have you noticed, Miss Maitland, that when two people are quite alike in some ways, they sometimes take pleasure in each other's misfortunes? That is how it is with my father and Jack, and I suppose it always will be. My father would have preferred to have had a daughter like you."

"Like me? I don't believe that he knows very much about me."

"He already has a very good opinion of you, gained from your father. He knows how much Mr. Maitland depends on you since the loss of your brother."

Julia was quite taken aback to find that tears came so quickly to her eyes at the mention of David's death, and even more upset to realise that her companion had noticed.

He now spoke in quite a different tone of voice. "Please forgive me, Miss Maitland, I do apologise for mentioning a subject so painful to you. I never met your brother, but I heard an account of the battle, passed on by your father from Freddie Brandon."

"It was not Freddie, but Dominic, the elder brother," Julia said quietly. "I know Freddie quite well, as he is the same age as his cousin Emily, who is a great friend of mine. She has lived with their family since her parents died. We are visiting the castle next week, although I don't know if Emily will be there."

"So that will not be the reason for your visit?"

"No, but my mother insists that we go. She is too easily impressed by people with titles, and she is very determined that I should be."

"We at least seem to have one thing in common then, Miss Maitland."

"What is that?"

"That we are both getting rather tired of other people trying to take control of our lives. I would guess, from the way you put it, that you are not anxious to marry the son of an earl?"

"Freddie is good fun, but of course he is the younger brother, and not the person that my mama has in mind for me." Then she remembered where she was, and why. "Should we not find out how your brother and Sophie are getting on down there?"

"Yes—you are quite right. If you will follow me, we can take another way from theirs, which is just as picturesque but not so likely to bring us to harm." And he suddenly gave her a warm smile, which made her feel rather breathless.

Perhaps fortunately, at that moment they came around a bluff and then had a better view of the two riders. Riding steadily down the slope, she followed her companion until they reached the stone wall where Jack Douglas was still untangling himself from the reins and muttering under his breath.

Sophie had turned her own mount on the far side of the wall, and was riding back towards Jack Douglas as Julia asked him how he was.

"I'm all right, Miss Maitland, just a bit winded," he said with more than a tinge of annoyance in his voice. "Your sister is a brave rider, and especially so on such a small mare."

He remounted his horse rather painfully, and they all continued together. Julia noticed that, from then on, he did not try so hard to impress Sophie with his riding prowess.

The rest of the outing was uneventful, and after about two hours they returned to the stables where Reuben the groom awaited them with a message from their host. A light collation was ready in the dining room, where Mr. Douglas and Mr. Maitland were anxious to start their meal without delay.

"Well, Miss Sophie," said her host, "have you enjoyed your ride, and meeting Jack and Kit?"

"Oh, yes, thank you so much, Mr. Douglas."

"And you, Miss Maitland? Have you enjoyed your visit?"

Julia acknowledged that she had had a very pleasant afternoon.

"Your father was telling me that you have been reading books about the improvements to farming practice being introduced by Mr. Coke in Norfolk? I had been hoping that Jack would travel to Holkham Hall for the same reason."

"I'm not interested," Jack said. "We are doing well enough the way we are running the farm now."

His father looked displeased. "Jack is not keen on anything new. You don't see it that way, Miss Maitland?"

"No, sir, for the changes to the farm that our manager has made since he went there, to learn about the best crop strains and changes to the types of stock that we should use, have made quite a difference to the income from our estate land."

"That is an unusual interest," interjected Kit Douglas.

Julia jibbed at this. "You mean for a young lady, Mr. Douglas?"

She could see from the amused expression in his eyes that she had scored a hit.

But his father answered for her. "Lewis tells me that Miss Maitland is doing her best to help him in her brother's place."

Kit looked chagrined. "I do apologise, Miss Maitland—please forgive me, for a moment I had forgotten your very sad circumstances."

"Perhaps you would not have me read books on that particular subject?" Julia said to him, with a wicked smile.

He acknowledged his error. "Touché, Miss Maitland! Are you going to confound me with my own remarks earlier this afternoon?"

"Although we shall not be able to stay on at Banford Hall after my father's cousin inherits the estate."

He nodded in understanding.

"You could say that I am wasting my time."

"I doubt very much if you ever waste your time, Miss Maitland."

Julia's father smiled at this, but suggested that they should be on their way home soon.

"I do hope that you will both come again," Mr. Douglas said, looking at his elder son. But Jack was too busy enjoying his plate of cakes and said nothing.

The journey back home was full of cheerful chatter between the sisters, whilst their father listened with approval. It was only when they entered the house that Julia suddenly remembered that she had left her old red shoes behind at the mansion.

TWO

Only an hour had passed on the following morning, but Julia was already feeling totally exhausted after trying to explain to her mother everything that had occurred during their visit to Norton Place.

Sophie, her mother's favourite, had already given a highly coloured account of their day, the excursion that the sisters had taken, with Jack riding with Sophie and Kit Douglas with Julia, and Sophie's success in jumping the wall when Jack's mount had refused.

As so often happened, Mama seemed to think that Julia had deliberately not ridden with Jack because she was being difficult, rather than it being the consequence of the headstrong way that Sophie had behaved.

"Mama, Jack Douglas is a really good horseman," said Sophie, "and we had such fun together out in the park."

Their mother was less interested in that than whether Julia had been able to have any private conversation with him.

"Mama," said Julia, "I have already tried to explain that I didn't ride with Jack Douglas, so I couldn't have any private conversation with him. But he didn't seem to be the kind of young man of whom you would approve."

"The visit was not arranged for you to decide whether I

would like the young man," her mother said in her dismissive way. "Papa made the journey so that you could have an opportunity to meet him."

Julia decided not to argue.

Her mother had always valued people with a title and inherited property above those who had made their own way in the world. Odd really, thought Julia, since Mama herself did not come from a long-established family.

"Harry Douglas is the kind of man who has always had to buy his own furniture."

"Buy his own furniture? Mama, what do you mean?" asked Sophie.

"A self-made man has not had the opportunity to inherit handsome furniture, or indeed an estate, from their parents or grandparents. They would have to buy such things themselves, Sophie."

"But what would Mr. Douglas have bought the Norton Place estate with, Mama? Did you not tell me that it is a very valuable property?"

"I've been told that his father was a farmer in only a small way of business. Harry Douglas bought Norton Place with money that he had made himself from trade. His late wife, whose father was a baronet, did have a handsome dowry, but Mr. Douglas himself does not come from a long-established family like the Brandons."

"If they are not a suitable family for us to associate with, why did we go to see Jack Douglas yesterday?" said Sophie.

"I did not say that they were an unsuitable family, Sophie, only that they were not long established. In any case, Papa particularly wanted Julia to go, and it was Mr. Douglas who suggested that you should accompany them. He has been a good friend to Papa, and he did his best to help us when we had the problem with the bank's failure."

"Jack did not seem to be very interested in Julia," said Sophie. "I thought that he liked me better!"

"He seemed to like animals much better than people in general," responded her sister.

Their mother decided to change the subject.

"Julia is going next week with Papa to meet Lord Brandon, the heir to the earldom. His family is very wealthy by inheritance, and would provide handsomely for the wife of their eldest son. As you know, Julia is already very friendly with his cousin Emily."

"I think," said Sophie, "that Julia likes Freddie, his brother, much better than she does Dominic."

"You," said her elder sister, "know nothing about it, and I would be grateful if you would mind your own business!"

For once, their mother frowned at Sophie and told her to keep quiet.

"What did you think of Jack's father, Harry Douglas?" said her mother.

"I liked him. He has a rather rough and ready way of speaking compared to many people that we know, but he seemed to be a fair-minded person, someone who could be relied upon in a difficult situation, and he was very understanding when referring to David. In fact, he was very pleasant to me in all our conversation."

Mama did not look impressed by this description.

"And the mansion and the park at Norton Place?"

Julia was beginning to feel rebellious at all this questioning. "It is a gracious house, quite large and very well kept, although perhaps missing a woman's touch in the furnishings. We only saw part of the park, but Sophie will have told you that there are extensive rides across the grounds."

"It is a pity," said her mother again, "that you did not ride with Jack Douglas rather than with his younger brother."

"You can blame that on Sophie, for it was she who rushed off soon after we got there to get her riding boots, and went off so quickly to the stables with Jack Douglas. That left me no choice but to go with his brother Kit. We had considerable difficulty in catching up with them."

Her mother, always unwilling to consider any fault in Sophie, frowned and was about to speak again when the housekeeper, Mrs. Andrews, came into the room.

"There is a package in the hall from Mr. Douglas for Miss Julia."

Mrs. Andrews had obviously been impressed by the messenger, for she ventured to add, "It was delivered by a tall young gentleman, ma'am."

"A package from Mr. Douglas, how exciting! What can it be?" said Sophie, rushing ahead of her sister towards the hall to inspect the parcel.

Julia, following more slowly with her mother, was puzzled. Why would Harry Douglas want to send her a package, and by a special messenger? She took the parcel—a neatly wrapped box—and carefully undid the ribbon and took off the paper wrapping.

Underneath, inside the silk-lined box, was a new pair of red leather shoes.

"Maybe they were sent by Jack Douglas!" exclaimed Sophie.

"I don't think that is very likely," said Julia, very quietly.

"How kind," said Mama, coming up behind them to look at the contents of the box. "Perhaps your old shoes could not be found? These are such good quality, and just the right size for you, Julia. I have to admit that they are a thoughtful gift."

Sophie looked disgruntled, for she felt that she was more than due for a new pair of shoes, and not her elder sister.

"I wish that I had lost my old shoes, then he would have sent some to me!"

Julia said nothing and, as soon as she could, put the shoes back in the box and slipped away to the privacy of her bedroom.

There, she sat on her bed and looked at the box. She lifted the lid and ran her hand around the lining of white figured silk. Then she lifted the shoes out, one by one, and put them on the bed cover. The smooth red leather was of the highest quality, and the shoes had been beautifully lined with grey silk, with a pale grey silk cord binding.

She looked at the shoes for a long time, running the tips of her fingers along the leather and turning them over and then back. Then she caught sight of a small folded piece of paper nestling on the silk inside the box. She picked it up and loosened the seal, unfolded the edges, and read the words written on the paper.

There was a short message in neat handwriting that said, "As I know that you like red shoes, I hope that you will accept these. They were made for a lady who did not have the chance to wear them. Thank you for visiting us yesterday."

Julia read, and then reread, the message. She recognized the writing. The gift had not come from Jack Douglas, or from his father. And from the description of the messenger, he had taken the trouble to deliver the shoes himself, since neither Jack nor his father could accurately be described as a tall young gentleman.

But Kit Douglas knew exactly where Julia had left her old shoes.

She had taken them off in the hall to put on her riding boots, and it was he who had given them to the butler for safekeeping. A servant could have been told to return them to her, so why had Kit Douglas not arranged that? And why had he wanted her to have these particular shoes, or decided to deliver them himself?

Julia folded the piece of paper neatly and put it back on the silk in the bottom of the box. Then she placed the shoes on top of the paper and replaced the lid on the top of the box.

Fortunately, it did not seem likely that either Sophie or their mother would realise what had happened, at least until someone mentioned the gift to Jack Douglas or to his father.

Or perhaps Mr. Douglas was already aware of the gift? It was all very puzzling.

Harriet, her youngest sister, was due back from school later that day, so Julia had little opportunity to reflect on the matter. Harriet was full of news about her friends at the school in Bath, and of the latest fashions being worn by the Ton in the city. She was keen to show off the new clothes that had been purchased for her by their maternal aunt, Lucy Harrison, a wealthy widow who lived in Bath.

Harriet opened the lid of her battered old school trunk, lifted the sheets of tissue paper hiding the clothes beneath, and revealed her new gowns. On top was a walking dress in soft green velvet, with looped sleeves and braided fastenings over an embroidered muslin skirt.

"Oh, Harriet," said Julia, "how fashionable you will look in your new green outfit! Is that just the latest thing in Bath? And everything matching—it's so delightful!"

Harriet took out some of the other things that her aunt had given her. There were two silk dresses, one in cream and one in grey, a beautiful pelisse edged with fur, some matching grey gloves in the softest leather, and a beautiful hat in cream felt trimmed with grey feathers.

"You may borrow some of my new things if you like, Julia," said Harriet, "for we are just the same size, and the colours will suit you."

That was the refreshing thing about Harriet, Julia reflected; she was always generous and cheerful, and never as thoughtless as Sophie could be.

"Perhaps I could wear your new green costume when I visit the Brandons at Cressborough Castle with Papa next week?"

"How grand to be visiting the Earl and Countess! But of course, Julia, you must look your best for that visit. Will you be seeing Freddie and Emily?"

"I think not," Julia replied. "In any case, the purpose of the visit is to meet Dominic, the elder brother. It is all part of Mama's great new plan to marry me off to someone wealthy and, if possible, with a title."

Harriet had not been at home when their parents had discussed with Julia what her future should be now that their family's fortune had been reduced and their father was unwell.

"Why? What great new plan? Have you had a formal invitation from the Earl and Countess, Julia?"

"Yes," said Julia in a puzzled tone. "I have asked Papa why they should consider me as a possible wife for Dominic, but he has no idea. Mama, as you can imagine, is overcome with delight, and considers the match already made. But Papa wants me to have more choice, so we have been to see the Douglas family, too."

"But Julia, you have always said that you would only marry for love! Even from Bath I have heard that Dominic Brandon leads such a wild life in London. And anyway, it was always Freddie that you liked best, not Dominic."

Julia sighed. "Freddie is the younger son, Harriet, and will only inherit a small income. Mama is determined that I should marry well, so that I can look after the two of you if anything happens to Papa."

"How dreadful!" cried Harriet. "Why did you have to agree to that?"

"I have not agreed to it, at least not yet. At present, I feel like a piece of meat in a shop window, being pushed and prodded by the customers before they decide which one will buy me." And Julia burst into tears.

"How dare they, Mama and Papa? Surely it is not necessary to you to be forced into a marriage that you don't want?"

Julia sniffed into her handkerchief, wiping the tears from her eyes before anyone else came into the room.

"We went yesterday to meet Papa's friend Mr. Douglas, and his elder son, Jack. Harry Douglas is very wealthy, and Mama says that I could marry his son instead. Their house, Norton Place, and the park are very grand. Sophie liked Jack Douglas and says that I should marry him. But, as you know, Sophie and I never agree about anything like that."

"I do hope that you do not have to choose between someone whom only Sophie likes, and a future earl who loses money at the gaming tables. Emily says that Dominic has some fancy ladies in keeping in London."

"Harriet!" said Julia. "What do you know about fancy ladies in London?"

"Quite a lot, because some of my school friends have brothers who know all about that," said Harriet without any trace of embarrassment. "In fact, some of them have older brothers who have fancy ladies of their own! But who wants to be married, even if her husband will become an earl, if he will never be at home, and never be faithful to you?"

Julia did not have an answer to that question, although she had asked it of herself many times over the past few weeks. What kind of choice did she have—between someone who seemed to like horses and farming better than people and a rake who preferred to live the high life in London, and who would expect her to socialise in the highest circles in the city, however boring that might be?

"Isn't there anyone else, Julia, who might offer for you? Our family has lived in this area so long, and we know so many people. Why aren't you allowed to choose for yourself?"

"The problem is money, Harriet. The failure of the bank in Derby means that we can now have only a small dowry each. And since David will not inherit the estate, we shall not be able to stay here if—that is when—something happens to Papa. Not every family wants their son to marry a young lady who is in that situation."

Clearly, Harriet had not realised this.

She should not have to worry about dowries and shortage of money, Julia thought. So she changed the subject, asking Harriet about her last term at school and about Aunt Lucy.

"Just think, Julia, no more school for me! Aunt Lucy says that I am quite the grown-up young lady now that I am sixteen."

Julia smiled at her. "Yes, even more grown-up than Sophie!"

"Yes, exactly, for you always say that Sophie acts like the baby of the family, and it's true."

"When you get to be twenty like me, you will find that you

do not always feel grown up, especially when things start going wrong in your life."

Harriet put down the dress that she had been holding and gave Julia a loving embrace. "It will turn out all right, you'll see! I'll make sure that it does."

With all the excitement of Harriet's return, Julia was tired when she went to bed that night and slept rather better than she had expected. After breakfast on the following morning, her father called her into his study.

"Julia, your mother tells me that a parcel came for you yesterday, from Mr. Douglas?"

Julia hesitated. She had never lied to her father and felt even less likely to do so now that he was unwell.

"Yes, the gift was a pair of new red shoes, like my old ones, but beautifully made, very expensive."

Her father looked at her with curiosity. He could sense from the tone of her voice that that was not the whole story.

"I have not told Mama, but I found a note at the bottom of the box."

He looked at the expression on her face, nearly said something, then did not.

She hesitated again, then added, "I do not believe that the gift came from Mr. Douglas."

"Why not? May I see the note?"

"Shall I fetch the box? It is in my room."

He paused. "No, perhaps it would be better if I came with you and saw it there."

They went upstairs along the wide corridor into her bedroom and closed the door. Julia opened her cupboard, removed the box from beneath the dress that she had laid on top to conceal it, and put it on the bed. Then she closed the cupboard and gave the box to him.

Her father took off the lid. He looked at the rich silk lining, and then took out one of the red shoes.

As Julia had done, he ran his hand along the smooth leather. He looked at her, smiled, then took out the other shoe and put both of them on her bed.

"So this is the note?" he said, looking at the piece of paper still in the box.

"Yes. Please read it." And she sat down on the bed and waited.

Her father read through the note slowly, and then read it again. He looked thoughtful. "No, this was not written by Harry Douglas. I would guess that the author is Kit?"

"Yes, I believe so. I recognized the writing—from the lists that he had made of the books in the library."

Her father looked at her warily, then said slowly, "Julia, young men do not normally give a valuable gift to young ladies whom they have only met on a single occasion."

"Yes, I know. And I guess that the shoes may have been made for his mother."

"Did Harry Douglas tell you that his wife had died just before Kit returned from Spain?"

"Yes."

"Julia, who knew where you had left your old shoes in Norton Place?"

"Kit Douglas gave them to the butler himself for safekeeping before we went out for our ride."

Her father looked out of the window for some time, then back at Julia.

"I am not sure quite what to say to you about this. He is the younger son, and you know very well that it is Jack who will inherit the estate. His father told me that Kit had joined the military hoping that he might make his way in the world, since he will only have a modest income otherwise. I would guess—you do not need to answer me—that you might like Kit much better than his elder brother. But it is Jack who could provide you with a secure future."

"All that you say is true, and I did like Kit better than Jack."

She felt tears welling in her eyes and fought to hold them back.

"Oh Papa, why cannot life go back to being like it was before the bank in Derby failed and then David was killed? Then I could have done as I want to, and marry whomever I like."

Her father answered the implied question. "Your mother only has your best interests at heart, and she is trying at the same time to secure the future of both your sisters."

Julia said nothing, for they had debated all this before, and it was all true. She felt that she was in a prison, with the gates about to close, and with no other options open to her.

Her father sat down beside her on the bed and took her hands in his, and they sat there side by side, and nothing was said for a short time.

Then the sound of voices in the distance reminded them that the rest of the family would be wondering where they were. She put the box back in its hiding place, her father took her hand, and they went downstairs.

"Papa, am I going with you and Julia to the castle next week?" demanded Sophie.

Her mother answered for him. "No, you have not been invited, only Julia will be going with Papa."

"But I would like to see Emily, for she is my friend as well as Julia's!"

"I understand that Emily may not be at home, but in any case that is not the purpose of the visit."

During the remainder of that week, Julia thought once or twice of telling Harriet about the note with the red shoes. It was not that her sister would tell Sophie anything, because Julia knew that Harriet was good at keeping secrets. It was more that Julia herself could not decide how she felt about the situation.

A message came from Mr. Douglas asking Julia and her father to visit him again in a few days' time. Sophie was miffed, for the note had made no reference to her at all. For once, Mama was happy about this, for she was determined that Julia should have some conversation with Jack Douglas without interruption.

Julia's father asked her in private whether she was happy to make a second visit to Norton Place. He would not have been surprised if she had refused. But she knew how he valued Harry Douglas's friendship and agreed to go, provided that it was after her visit to the castle to see the Brandons.

Meanwhile, Mama was anxious to make sure that Julia was clear about how she should behave when she met the Earl and Countess.

Julia had been to Cressborough Castle many times, for she had been to school with Emily in York and had met her uncle and aunt before. Through Emily, she had become friendly with Freddie Brandon. Dominic, his brother, was more than five years older and had been away at university and then in the army for most of the time when Julia had visited Emily.

Since then, as Harriet had reminded her, he had been living in the family house in London, and by all accounts had joined the fast gaming set and was living the high life in town.

Julia imagined that her mother was aware of all of this, but was equally certain that it would not deter her from encouraging the match with Dominic Brandon because of the financial advantages attached.

The day before the visit to the castle, Mama decided to make quite sure that everything was ready. Julia always disliked fuss, and she could see that the next few hours were going to be very tedious. She could have done everything herself, but Mama was determined to be involved in every single detail.

"Have you decided what you're going to wear tomorrow, Julia? I know that you are very fond of your blue dress, but it is really getting rather shabby at the back. Don't you think that it might be better to wear something else?"

Julia suspected that it would not make much difference what she replied to this question, for it was very likely that, as usual, her mother had already made up her mind.

"Harriet says that you may borrow the green costume given to her by Aunt Lucy, so I hope that you will agree to that kind offer, for it is a colour that is so becoming to you."

Julia did not argue. She had no intention of wearing her new red shoes, and even her mother could not possibly insist that they matched the proposed outfit better than her black ones.

"I think you said, Julia, that Lord Brandon bought himself out of the regiment at the end of last year?"

"Yes, I don't think that soldiering was much to his taste. Emily said, last time I saw her, that Freddie will probably carry on, for he hopes for promotion, and the war with Napoléon is far from being won."

Julia had often wondered whether it would not have been better if her mother had succumbed to her grief when the news of David's death came last year. She had not been surprised at herself or her father, who had wept most of their tears in private, but usually her mother, like Sophie, did not conceal her feelings in any situation. It must have been a second devastating blow for her to know that she was going to lose the house after Papa's death, and would then have a much reduced income.

It was as if Julia had spoken these thoughts aloud.

"Julia, did Freddie Brandon ever mention David's death to you? I wished at the time that he had told us more about what happened."

"No, Mama, he didn't. He only knew what Dominic had told him."

When the next day came, her mother busied herself in making sure that all the details of Julia's outfit were perfect, her shoes shined to the highest gloss, her hair washed and dressed in the most becoming ringlets, and everything done so that her eldest daughter was looking her best.

Even Sophie agreed that Julia looked rather fine in the green dress—if she was careful, Harriet might agree to lend the dress to her as well. Julia was not the only person who looked good in green.

Harriet gave Julia a big hug, and whispered in her ear, "Don't let them make you agree to anything that you don't want to do. He's not the only rich young man in the world, and certainly not the nicest."

Julia had to laugh at her sister's determination.

"With you on my side, Harriet, I'm sure everything will be all right!"

Mama looked puzzled, but her father gave her an understanding smile. Knowing Harriet as he did, he could guess what she might have said. His youngest daughter was always a person to be reckoned with in a difficult situation. It was very helpful that she had finished with school and could offer Julia some much needed support.

Julia was just about to say good-bye to her sisters when the housekeeper came into the drawing room in great excitement.

"Mrs. Maitland, ma'am, the Earl's barouche is at the door for Miss Julia!"

There was a stunned silence for several moments, and only Papa showed no surprise.

When Julia realised this, she said, "You knew—why didn't you tell me?"

Papa smiled. "Because I thought that it would be pleasant news—and it appears that I was right. A message came from the castle for me last night that, if the weather were to be fine today, the Earl would send his open carriage for us to enjoy the drive."

THREE

There, waiting at the door, was a handsome open barouche, the gleaming coachwork painted in the deepest blue and with the heraldic crest of the Brandon family in the centre of each door. The metalwork had been polished to a mirrorlike shine, and the coachman was dressed in the Brandon livery, seated on the front box behind a pair of the finest greys.

For once, Sophie was speechless at this magnificent sight.

Behind her, Mama exclaimed with delight.

"Julia, how wonderful, and how kind of the Brandons to send the carriage for you and Papa!"

Papa looked at Julia with a quiet smile, but said nothing. Julia herself had to admit that the barouche was very impressive, and waited for the driver to assist her into the carriage. Papa followed, seating himself opposite her on the deeply buttoned leather seat with his back to the horses.

Harriet came forward from the front door of the house and, leaning over the door of the barouche, whispered in Julia's ear, "How very grand, but don't forget what I said!"

Julia laughed out loud. "No, but you must admit that we shall be travelling in style!"

The driver gathered his horses, and they were soon on their way.

"Papa, why do you think that the Earl has taken the trouble

to send the barouche—to be so kind to me? I know that we have spoken about this before, but I really cannot think of any reason for him to single me out from all the other young ladies who would like to marry his heir."

"I really have no idea—I can only suggest that, if you have the opportunity, you should ask him that yourself whilst we are at the castle."

Julia considered the matter for a few moments. She had met the Earl before, and he was not a particularly difficult person to converse with. But it was surely not good manners to raise that subject on such a visit. On the other hand, how else was she to find out? She could ask Dominic, and maybe he was more likely to give an honest reply. Or perhaps he had had nothing to do with it.

At least, for now, she was enjoying the drive on such a nice day, and it was not too long before the castle came into view. The high stone walls were an impressive sight, built on a rocky bluff rising above them, with no apparent entry point. The entrance towers only came into view once they had passed across the river bridge, rounded the bend in the road, and found themselves facing the portcullis and the gates into the courtyard.

They were received with due ceremony at the main doors, and the butler led the way to the central hall, with its high domed roof painted with colourful frescoes of biblical scenes. There they were met by a footman, again resplendent in the Brandon livery, who announced them at the door of the main salon.

"Mr. Maitland and Miss Maitland."

Seated on a large chaise longue on the far side of the room was the Earl himself, whilst the Countess and her son were side by side in chairs opposite him. They all rose, and the introductions were made. Polite inquiries were made about Mrs. Maitland's health and about Sophie and Harriet.

"I regret, Julia, that Emily is not at home," said the Countess. "She is still away staying with friends and will not be back until next week. Freddie also asks to be excused, since he is away on military duties."

"I am sorry not to see them, but I hope that there will be another opportunity soon."

"But you know Dominic, of course," said the Earl. "Although he is often in town, he has promised me that, now that he has left the regiment, he will spend more time here at the castle helping me manage the estate."

Julia looked directly at Dominic for the first time, and was relieved to see that he smiled cautiously in return. He was as she had remembered him, rather taller than Freddie, but with the same thick dark hair and strongly marked brows above deep blue eyes. His coat and breeches were appropriate for a day in the country, but so expertly cut that they could only have been made for him by one of the best tailors in London.

"He would like to show you the picture gallery," continued the Earl, "so why don't you go there now, before we take some refreshments with your father."

The tone in which this comment was made did not seem to invite discussion, so Julia followed Dominic out of the room and through a series of grand salons to the gallery. Both walls were lined with oil paintings, which seemed to Julia to extend as far as the eye could see.

"I am, you will have noticed, burdened with rather too many ancestors, Miss Maitland."

Julia was comforted by this remark, remembering that he shared Freddie's lively sense of humour.

"I suppose that applies to everyone, though not all end up in an oil painting! Are there any portraits of your parents?"

"Not here; you can see their likenesses on the west wall in the dining room. It is a family tradition that the paintings in the gallery are only of Brandons who have moved on to the next life."

Julia smiled. "Some of your ancestors seem to have had very large families." She regretted making the remark almost as soon as she had uttered it.

"Do you like children, Julia? I fear that I will be expected to produce an heir in the next generation as quickly as possible, once I am married."

This reference to the underlying reason for her visit immediately removed her enjoyment of their conversation, and she was silent.

Moving to stand by one of the tall windows, he drummed his fingertips on the sill in a nervous manner. "I must ask you—do you favour our suggested alliance with any enthusiasm?"

Julia had considered already what her reply to this question might be. Perhaps this was her opportunity to ask why she was being considered as his prospective bride.

"Dominic, please tell me, honestly, why should you wish to marry me? You must be one of the most eligible young men in town at present, with every fond mama keen to throw their daughters at your feet!"

He laughed, and said, "You are right, and a damned tiresome business it is, I can assure you. Your brother saved my life in Spain, and I had promised him when he got to Spain that I would look after you if anything happened to him. You were David's favourite sister, you know."

"Thank you. But if everyone married as a result of such circumstances, there would be some very odd alliances in the world.

There are other ways, no doubt, in which you could offer me assistance, should I need it?"

"True. But consider the situation from my point of view. We know each other a little already, since you are a friend of my brother and, of course, my cousin Emily. I have to marry someone soon, to continue the family line—my parents insist on that—but so many of the eligible girls are so vapid and boring. My parents like you, and certainly prefer you to some of the other candidates for the role who are pushing themselves forward."

He observed her startled expression. "You may think that too cold-hearted a way of considering the matter, but I know you to be an intelligent and sensible person, aware of how family life is conducted in the highest circles."

He meant, she assumed, by that last remark that she would have to turn a blind eye to any liaisons that he might conduct in town outside his marriage, and the time that he might spend at the various gaming houses and in his clubs drinking with his friends.

"I am not sure that that is the kind of life that I would like, however comfortable the financial circumstances that I might be offered."

"If you would prefer to spend most of your time here at the castle, I would not object to that. It is a good place to raise children."

Julia's dismayed expression did not escape him.

"That is not the kind of marriage you would want? You had hoped to marry for love? Not many people are that fortunate."

"No, but I would much prefer to be together with my husband for most of the time, to share common interests."

"Not many relationships stay like that in the highest social circles, Miss Maitland, at least in the long run."

JULIA AND THE MASTER OF MORANCOURT

"No, I accept that."

"I sense that you do not approve of my suggestion of your living here whilst I would be in London. My parents have been married for thirty years and seem to have found that a tolerant attitude to each other's preferences works for them. It has been a comfortable basis for their relationship."

Julia wondered if that was more his father's view than his mother's, since the Earl had had a reputation for fast living when in town, and not only in his youth.

"I am trying to be honest with you, if only for your brother's sake."

"I am grateful to you for that, Dominic."

She turned away to look out of the window. She was aware that many young women would be only too happy to accept an offer from the heir to the earldom, and to be assured of wealth and a great social position for the rest of their lives. Her mother had already told her how lucky she was to be offered such an opportunity when she now had only a small dowry and no share in property or the family estate.

"I do not need an answer now, Julia. A few weeks' delay will make no difference. Why don't we meet again, once you have had the opportunity to consider the matter more thoroughly? My offer still stands in the meantime."

Julia thanked him. She should be grateful, she supposed, for his being thoughtful enough not to rush her. Whether she wanted someone to marry her because of a promise made to her brother was quite a different matter.

They returned to the salon, where her father was apparently enjoying his conversation with the Earl and Countess.

"Well, Miss Maitland, what do you think of all those past

Brandons?" said the Earl in a friendly tone. "Some of the earlier ones would make good brigands, don't you think! We are lucky that they are not still alive, in my opinion!"

Matching his mood, Julia said, "No more than many families may have had in their past history, sir. But I was glad to have been able to see more of the castle. On my visits to see Emily and Freddie, we usually spend most of our time in your family's private quarters."

"Yes, these rooms here are shown to visitors when we are not in residence. We spend most of our family time elsewhere in the castle." Then, turning to her father, he said, "Lewis, shall we go and look at those bank papers now, so that I can sign them for you before we leave?"

Her father answered Julia's unspoken question before she could say anything.

"I brought them with me at the Earl's suggestion—it is just some unfinished business," and he left the room with their host before she could reply.

"Come and sit next to me, Julia," said the Countess. "And Dominic, please go and find Annette, and ask her to bring down the blue silk shawl that I have set aside for Miss Maitland."

To Julia she added, "Annette Labonne is my personal attendant. She was born in northern France and, before she became my dresser, Annette was our nursery maid when Dominic and Freddie were young."

Julia hesitated after he had gone out of the room, but only for a moment.

"Ma'am, would you find me presumptuous if I asked you a personal question?"

"If I did, I need not answer you."

Julia took this as being an affirmative.

"Dominic said just now that you had spent part of your

married life living here with the children whilst the Earl was more in town—were you happy with that arrangement?"

The Countess did not answer immediately, but then said, "I would prefer to reply by saying that Dominic is, in some respects, very like his father. I would expect that he would want to adopt that pattern of life—yes, my dear. If that would make you unhappy, you should not marry him. But if you fear that he would in any way be disrespectful to you in public if you were to become his wife, you can put that idea out of your head!"

"Thank you for answering. I apologise for any intrusion."

The Countess took Julia's hand and held it firmly. "Marriage is not always a happy state, my dear, but I am sure from what Emily and Freddie have told me that you would make Dominic as happy as anyone of our personal acquaintance."

Anyone of our personal acquaintance—that struck Julia as being a rather unusual expression.

The Countess smiled at Julia. "I never had a daughter of my own, so the untimely death of Emily's parents gave me an opportunity to care for the daughter that I would have otherwise been denied. I would be happy to welcome you also into our household."

It would, Julia thought to herself, be so very much easier to reject the idea of marriage with Dominic if she disliked him, or either of his parents, more.

Dominic returned with the shawl, which the Countess insisted on giving to Julia, saying that it would flatter her colouring. As she gratefully accepted this generous gift, her father returned to the salon with their host.

The Earl summoned the footman to have the barouche brought round to the front door, and Julia and her father said their farewells and were escorted to the carriage.

They had travelled some distance on their return journey in silence before Julia said, "Papa, there is no connection between your signing those papers and the suggestion that I should marry Dominic—is there?"

"No, my dear, I promise you that there is none. The documents relate to guarantees that were offered by the Earl to help me when I had difficulties following the failure of the bank in Derby. He also had losses, but they were minor in the context of his overall investments. He assisted me by giving the guarantees, which I have now been able to discharge."

"Papa, I cannot understand the reason that Dominic gave me for his proposal that I should marry him."

"What reason was that?"

"That he had promised David in Spain that he would look after me."

"I would agree that a proposal of marriage would certainly be an extreme reaction to such a request. It is not as though you are in very reduced circumstances, or have no one to look after you."

"Exactly, Papa. It does not make sense. I am going to speak to either Freddie or Emily as soon as they get back, for surely one of them can tell me more."

"It is not that you really dislike Dominic, is it? He is really quite a pleasant young man."

"Yes, indeed he is. But he is also used to doing exactly as he pleases, and living the high life in town. That is not unusual when you have been the heir to such riches all your life. No, it is not that. I just do not want to live in London, or move in the highest circles, where people are competing with one another all the time. Not everyone is as pleasant as the Earl and Countess. I'm sorry, Papa, but I do not wish to be in that kind of gilded cage for the rest of my life."

Her father looked rueful, and then replied, "Say nothing to your mother as yet. She has pinned such hopes on that alliance, and indeed would much prefer it to your marrying Jack Douglas. Let's wait and see what happens."

Sophie and Harriet ran out of the house to greet them as soon as they heard the carriage enter the drive at home. They were both full of questions about how the day had gone, of what Julia had seen, of who had been there, and about every detail of who had said what to whom.

Mama also wanted a full description of how the Earl and Countess had received Julia and her father, and what the outcome of the visit had been.

Between them, Julia and Papa gave what explanations they could, although she decided that it was best not to communicate all the details of her conversation with Dominic Brandon to anyone.

"Mama, the Countess told me that Emily will be back from Bath quite soon, and I have left a message asking her to come over here as soon as she is ready to do so."

Meanwhile, her mother had not forgotten that Papa and Julia were to make a return visit to see Mr. Douglas and Jack on the following day. Sophie was still sulking about not being included in the party, but Harriet promised to let her try on some of the new garments given to her by Aunt Lucy, which was some consolation.

This time, the journey to Norton Place did not seem to Julia to take so long, and the carriage wheels were soon rolling up the drive towards the mansion. They were greeted in a friendly fashion as before, and this time Jack was waiting with his father at the top of the steps. He was dressed more smartly in a tweed jacket above dark green riding breeches and well-polished boots.

"I have told Jack here," said Mr. Douglas, "that he is to show Miss Maitland how he can make proper polite conversation during this visit, and that he is not to mention a horse, or anything to do with farming, in the first thirty minutes!"

Julia had to smile at this, though she felt sorry for the red-faced young man.

They all went along into the drawing room, and she was placed opposite Jack and next to Harry Douglas. There was an awkward silence, so Julia decided that she should say something before her host criticised his son again.

"Perhaps, Jack, I ought to start our conversation, since your father is trying to make it so difficult for you."

She had meant to be making a joke, but Jack merely looked rather embarrassed, and said nothing in reply.

Julia tried again. "We went to the castle yesterday to see the Brandons, but it is a much less friendly house than this. Have you been there, Jack?"

"No, I don't think so."

"My sister Sophie sends her regards to you. Our younger sister, Harriet, has finished at school in Bath now and is back home with us. Have you met her?"

"No," said Jack.

By this time, Mr. Douglas's irritation was becoming obvious. He clearly was not impressed at his son's conversational skills.

"Jack, why don't you tell Miss Maitland about our visit to the spa at Buxton last week?"

Jack mumbled something that Julia didn't catch. Her father decided to help her out.

"Perhaps it would be better, Harry, if we did let Jack talk about horses or the farm, for those are the things that he likes best?"

Jack looked relieved, and for a few minutes he gave a creditable account of his activities riding on the estate and supervising the farm workers. It was the first time since they had met that Julia felt it possible to have anything in common with Jack Douglas. But it was hardly a sound foundation for a relationship to be able only to converse on subjects of minor interest to her.

She had been hoping that Kit Douglas would appear, but there was no sign of him. Julia had agreed with her father before they arrived that neither of them would mention the gift of the new red shoes. Before Julia could put the question herself, her father enquired about the whereabouts of Kit.

"He has been called away at short notice to his godmother's bedside. The message came three days ago that she is very seriously ill. She is a distant relative of my late wife. We have not yet had any further news from Kit of how she is."

Jack did not seem to be very interested in this situation, and he began to fidget as he sat beside his father. Julia was beginning to think that they had stayed long enough, despite the obvious anxiety of their host that his son should show himself in a better light.

Perhaps fortunately, Reuben entered the room at that point to ask that Jack should return to the farmyard where an emergency had arisen.

"Of course you must go," said Julia's father immediately. "Thank you for sparing the time to see us, Jack."

Jack nodded and made his escape so rapidly that Julia wondered whether he had made a prior arrangement to be called away.

"Well, Miss Maitland," said their host, "how did you find your visit to the castle? We are not such grand folks here as they are."

Julia caught his joking mood, and smiled in reply. She had

thought of the possibility that Mr. Douglas knew that a competing suitor was being proposed for her hand, and she did not want him to feel at a disadvantage in that situation.

"For grand folks," she said, "they are not at all puffed up or unpleasant. But that formal kind of life doesn't suit everyone. And unfortunately Emily and her younger cousin Freddie were away, so we couldn't see them."

"Well," said her father, "perhaps we should be on our way now, Harry, or my wife will begin to wonder what has become of us. Please give our regards to your younger son when he returns home. I hope that there is better news of his godmother."

And with that they rose and were about to say good-bye to their host when the butler entered the room and spoke in an undertone to Mr. Douglas. He turned to Julia and said in a friendly tone, "I am reminded that we must return the red shoes that were left here during your last visit, Miss Maitland."

She said simply, "Thank you, sir."

Then her father said farewell to his friend and, collecting the shoes from the butler in the hall, they both went down the steps to their carriage.

On the way home, Julia acknowledged to herself that the main reason that she had agreed to the visit was in the hope of seeing Kit Douglas again. She had an odd, empty feeling in her stomach that would not go away, and even a happy greeting from her sisters on their return home did not help much.

Over the next few days, Julia was well aware that her parents were having various conversations about the visits to Norton Place and to the Brandons at the castle, but they said nothing to her. She tried to keep busy, entertaining Sophie and Harriet and hoping that either Emily or Freddie would come to call soon.

At last, the urgent knock on the door came, announcing the arrival of Emily, full of news of her stay with friends near Leeds, and of Freddie's progress in the regiment. Her golden curls were tumbling in an unruly fashion beneath a most becoming new bonnet trimmed with pink ribbon to match her dress, and she carried a pink reticule to match.

"Oh, Julia," she said "it was such a pity that you were not able to travel with me, for we would have had such a good time together. When I go there next, you must come with me, for there are so many handsome young men in that part of York-shire, and the balls and musical evenings are held every week in Leeds!"

Julia felt like saying that she was rather tired of being part of the marriage market, even in a small way in Derbyshire, but her friend was so encouraging that perhaps she was being too cynical. Sophie and Harriet made it very clear that, if Julia didn't want to go, they would be delighted to accompany Emily on her next visit. However their enthusiasm was dampened by Mama pointing out that they were too young to go without her. Eventually, Julia had the chance to talk to Emily in private about her discussion with Dominic Brandon.

"Emily, what I cannot understand is why your cousin should want to offer for me just because he made a promise to my brother before he died. I am sure that there is something else that I don't know or that someone is not telling me. Can you help?"

"Well, after Dominic bought himself out of the regiment, he went back to live in our town house in London and resumed his normal life—I have told you about that before—enjoying the company of 'bits of muslin,' as he would call it, and gaming in the clubs such as Whites or Brooks's with his friends."

Julia nodded—none of that came as any surprise to her.

"Perhaps I shouldn't really tell you, but as your good friend I ought to. A few weeks ago, Freddie found out that Dominic had fallen in love with a very beautiful girl—the sister of one of his gaming friends in town. But she has already had a child with someone else, and my parents will not hear of his marrying her. Dominic has told Freddie that he has nothing to lose by a marriage with you, provided that you would not object in his continuing to see her in private when he is in London."

"Oh! So that is why he wanted me to know that your aunt and uncle had led partly separate lives. And the Countess hinted to me that Dominic was likely to want to live in the same way the as his father has done."

"You wouldn't agree to that, would you, Julia?"

"Not if I had any choice in the matter!"

"Nor would I. Who would want to be treated as second best!"

"Mama would say that we are being unrealistic. After all, many people that we know live like that. Not everyone has a choice, Emily. You may have a handsome dowry but, the way things are now with Papa's estate, Mama says that I can't be so choosy."

Emily was about to say something soothing, but remembered that Julia might be right and kept quiet.

"I can see now why your aunt and uncle are very anxious for Dominic to marry, and that they prefer someone they already know. After all, they are rich enough not to worry about a large dowry."

"Yes, that's true."

"And they are hoping that his liaison in town with that girl will wither away?"

"It is very much more likely that, if it did wither away, he would start another relationship with someone else who was equally unsuitable!" said Emily. "Harriet is quite right. You should do as you like, Julia, and not allow your parents, or anyone else, to tell you who you should marry."

FOUR

Since this information had been given to her in confidence, Julia did not pass it on to her father. Papa seemed very anxious at present to distract her from any thoughts connected with engagement or marriage. She knew that he was worrying about her and that couldn't be good for his health. Mama was still insisting that Julia couldn't possibly refuse the opportunity to become the next Countess of Cressborough, and clearly she thought that a marriage with a son of the Douglas family was quite beneath Julia's consideration by comparison, although she was not saying that in front of Papa.

Julia had tried to find out from her father whether there had been any news of Kit Douglas's returning to Norton Place, but it seemed that he was still away.

She had not said much to Emily about her visit there, or about Kit. She was not sure enough of her own feelings to do so, and in any case she knew that Mama would strongly oppose her taking any interest in someone who had such limited prospects.

The days seemed to drag by. Fortunately, her mother was kept busy with entertaining Sophie and Harriet and looking after Papa, so Julia tried to avoid any conversation with her mother about either Jack Douglas or Dominic Brandon. Quite often, she was able to escape to the library to read a book and forget about anything to do with engagements or marriage.

Emily came from the castle again to gossip about the latest fashions and to bring the news from Freddie in London. She said that Dominic was living in the town house, too, but Freddie did not seem to be seeing very much of him.

The following week her father called her into the library to say he had a reply to a letter that he had sent to Aunt Lucy in Bath.

"You will see that she has invited you to stay for a few weeks, and I do encourage you to go, for the change of scene would be good for you." He sighed, and added, "Your mother would not agree with me, but you need to get away from all this fuss for a while at least."

He observed her cautious expression. She knew that some people regarded Bath as one of the best places to find a husband for their daughters. That was the last thing that she needed at present.

"I am not trying to order you to go, Julia, but please think about the offer carefully before you refuse. You would meet new people and Bath is a very different world from rural Derbyshire."

When she visited Emily a few days later, her friend was all in favour of the idea. She was very fond of Bath, and suggested that they could travel together in the Brandons' carriage to the family's London house. They could stay there for a few days in town, and see Freddie, before Julia continued with Emily to stay with Aunt Lucy in Bath.

So she decided to accept the invitation, and wrote to Aunt Lucy to ask if Emily could stay with her for a week or so.

As usual, Emily got everybody organised to suit herself. Julia was not involved at all in making the arrangements, but her friend persuaded the Earl and Countess to make the travelling carriage available so that the two young ladies could be transported to London. Harriet helped Julia pack, but she did not take her new red shoes—they were too precious to risk losing them.

It was clear to Julia that Mama was hoping that the stay in town at the Brandons' house would encourage an engagement with Dominic. Luckily, there was no need yet for Julia to make it clear to her mother that that was the last thing she wanted.

She did find it very difficult to leave her father behind at home, for he was clearly ailing and spent much of the time sitting quietly in his chair in the library, reading a favourite book.

"Promise me, Papa, that you will look after yourself properly whilst I'm away. Harriet has said that she will take care of you for me, but please try to rest as much as you can."

Her father patted her hand, telling her not to worry too much about him, and wishing her a pleasant stay with her aunt.

"Make sure, Julia," said Mama, "that you take full advantage of your stay with Emily in London. It's not often that you will have the opportunity, and I'm sure that Dominic or Freddie Brandon will be willing to escort you to the theatre and other delights."

The journey to town passed pleasantly enough in Emily's company, and on the third day the carriage entered the square and drew up outside the Brandons' town house.

There seemed to Julia to be just as many staff there as at the castle, and a bewildering number of footmen and maids ran around getting the trunks from the carriage and taking them away upstairs.

The butler coughed discreetly to attract their attention.

"There is a message for you, Miss Emily, from Mr. Freddie. He will be able to leave his military duties this evening to escort you both to see Mr. Joseph Grimaldi at the Sadler's Wells

Theatre. He said that you are not to wait dinner for him, but he promises to be back in good time."

Then one of the footmen took Julia and Emily to the bedrooms that had been prepared for them.

The house, though not as large or as grand as the castle in Derbyshire, seemed to Julia to be like a palace, with rich drapes on every window, elaborate furniture, and carefully chosen colours decorating the walls and high ceilings. Julia's clothes seemed to occupy only a very small corner of the enormous cupboard in her room, and the bed was vast, with the softest mattress she had ever encountered. From their bedrooms, there were good views over the square at the front of the house and, at the back, the house had an outlook over the large private garden.

Freddie was as good as his word and came rushing in that evening to change, ready to take them to the Sadler's Wells Theatre. During the journey across town in the Brandons' carriage, he gossiped about life in the city, the many entertainments available for the visitor, and the places of interest that they were passing along the streets.

Mr. Grimaldi was the most expressive clown that Julia had ever seen. His face was painted with a coloured triangle on each cheek and that, along with all his facial contortions and athletic visual tricks, kept his audience on tenterhooks throughout his performance. To her surprise, he encouraged the audience to join in by shouting out, and Freddie did so, although Emily and Julia were content to watch the fun. Julia tried to store everything in her memory, so that she could tell Sophie and Harriet all about it when she got home.

On their journey back to the square, Julia took the opportunity to ask Freddie about Dominic's account of what had occurred in Spain during the war.

"I don't think that my brother is very proud of what happened," he said.

"Why is that, exactly?" asked Julia.

"Well, as you know, Dominic and David were in the same regiment in Spain. My brother was with his men outside the fortress at Badajoz, waiting for the assault on the French to begin. His commanding officer knew that he had been in the area before, and asked him to be ready early the next morning to lead a group through very dangerous terrain towards breaches already made in the castle walls. That night, as usual, he had been drinking heavily with his friends. The following morning when he was roused from sleep by his servant, he was much too drunk to get out of his bed."

"Oh," said Julia, "how dreadful!"

"It is not so unusual," said Freddie, "for officers to get drunk the night before a military advance, but not that drunk. Anyway, his commanding officer realised that somebody else would have to lead the assault. So he asked David to go instead, although he did not know the locality at all. But your brother agreed to go in Dominic's place."

Julia could just imagine David doing that; he would have been keen to get involved in the action as soon as possible.

"When your brother left the camp with his men and they began to make their way up a narrow gully towards the rear of the fortress, an enormous mine left by the French soldiers exploded. They were all killed instantly."

Julia closed her eyes for a few moments—it was so easy to imagine, and so very painful.

"Dominic told me afterwards that, if he had led the patrol

himself, he would have kept to the higher ground, because he knew that mining a gully was a favourite French tactic. But he had not been able to remind David about that because he was so drunk that morning."

"So," said Julia slowly, "Dominic feels guilty about my brother's death because if he had not been drunk, he would have led the troops himself; or if he had told my brother about the French practice of laying mines, David would be alive today? Oh, now I see."

"As you can imagine, his commanding officer was not at all happy about what had happened at Badajoz. It wasn't the first time that Dominic's behaviour had caused problems. When my brother returned to London, he decided that army life was not for him, and he bought himself out of his commission as soon as he could."

He hesitated. "Emily, did you tell Julia about Dominic and Christina?"

She nodded. "I did, a little, but not everything."

"Since he came back to town, I suspect that Dominic has been seeing the girl again regularly, without my parents' knowledge. You probably know that they will not allow an engagement, but they can't stop him from doing as he likes whilst he's in London. And I guess that he is losing so much money at the gaming tables that he must be in dun territory, very short of money, but I can't do anything about that."

It is just as well, thought Julia, that Freddie and Emily are such good friends of mine, so that I know about all this. Otherwise, I could have been pushed by Mama into marriage with Dominic in ignorance of everything, and found myself in a very difficult situation for the rest of my life. Indeed, I still could. Mama believes that anyone with a title is a worthwhile catch as a husband, however unfaithful he would be.

In her bedroom that night, Julia thought about what she had learnt. It seemed to be very unlikely that the information about Dominic's behaviour in Spain would be of any consolation to her mother, and nothing could bring David back. It might, she reflected, be in her own interest for her mother's opinion of Dominic to be damaged, but she would have to keep that idea to herself as a last resort.

The following morning, the two young ladies went shopping at Wilding and Kent in New Bond Street for fabric to have made up into new gowns when they returned to Derbyshire.

"The Countess has told me to charge her account with a length of French silk for you as well," said Emily.

Julia demurred, not only embarrassed at this unexpected generosity, but anxious not to do anything that might imply a closer connection with Dominic Brandon.

Her friend was not deceived. "Julia, the Countess is very generous, and would not want me to purchase for myself without getting something for you. Forget about Dominic, this has nothing to do with him."

"Can you tell me, please, whether this is genuine French silk?" Emily asked the assistant.

"Of course, Madam, all our silk fabrics are French."

Julia chose a length of pale blue, and it was not until they had taken their purchases and were on the way to the carriage that her friend continued, "What that girl didn't say was that the silk must have been smuggled into the country, because of the blockade in the Channel."

"Oh!" said Julia, horrified. "Should we have been buying something illegal?"

"Everybody else does, so why not us?" said Emily, quite unconcerned.

Freddie had a business appointment in the afternoon, but he had arranged for the carriage to take the two friends to Somerset House in the Strand, where the Royal Society's annual exhibition of paintings was on display.

"There are said to be nearly a thousand pictures on the walls this year," said Emily, "although with this throng of people we shall be lucky to see a tenth of them!"

Julia silently agreed, for the noise and hubbub were so great that she could hardly hear her friend speak. For people of quality, there was a great deal of pushing and shoving going on in the galleries, so that the busy road outside seemed quite peaceful when they finally emerged and found the carriage waiting for them in a side street.

To celebrate their last night in London, Freddie had been persuaded by Emily to take them to the famous Vauxhall Gardens. Julia had heard so much about these pleasure walks and entertainments. They both put on their best evening attire, Emily in pink and Julia in palest green. Freddie wore his full regimentals and looked very grand. It cost them a full two shillings to enter, which he kindly paid for each of them.

The gardens were alongside the river and were planted with beautiful trees arranged in lines. On the paths around the gardens was every kind of person—people of quality walking in groups, all dressed in the latest fashion, but also ladies whose raiment proclaimed them to be looking for more intimate attention from the many young single gentlemen roaming the paths, seeking an assignation for the night. Julia was glad that they had Freddie to escort them.

There were musical groups playing in each corner, illuminated fountains, fireworks, and magicians performing tricks to deceive the eye. Freddie said that the gardens attracted people from all levels of society, from English royalty to shop boys and their sweethearts. In between the musical events, people paraded along the walks in their finery.

Turning a corner, Emily suddenly exclaimed, "Isn't that Dominic over there, under those trees?"

They all peered across the throng and saw that it did indeed appear to be Dominic. He was dressed in the height of fashion and had his arm around the waist of a willowy blond beauty wearing a diaphanous pink muslin dress topped by a fur tippet, and displaying a great deal of expensive-looking jewellery.

"Is that Christina, do you think? What a beautiful dress! It is so elegant," said Emily.

"Yes," said Freddie shortly. "Probably a very expensive garment, and rather too revealing if you ask me. Come, let's go a different way." And he led them in another direction along the gravel path under the lanterns.

They took refreshments in one of the supper boxes that Freddie had reserved overlooking the orchestra. After that, they did not stay too late, for the carriage was to leave for Bath early on the following morning.

Julia and Emily said good-bye to Freddie rather anxiously, as he was due to rejoin his regiment and leave for Spain within a few days. Emily was rather quiet for the first few miles of the journey, and Julia suspected that she was thinking of the difficulties that might lie ahead for her cousin on the Continent. There didn't seem to be any very effective way of consoling her, except by saying that Freddie was one of those lucky people who always seemed to survive anything.

"Do you know," said Emily, changing the subject firmly, "what entertainments your aunt has in mind for us in Bath?"

"Not yet. As Aunt Lucy has no children of her own, she

always spoils us when we stay with her, which is so very kind. Look at all the nice things that she bought for Harriet at the end of her time at school. She is very generous, but I expect that she really enjoys having someone to fuss over. What I do fear is that she will want to introduce me to every eligible young man in Bath. I really would like not to have to think about marriage at all whilst I'm there."

"I have told my aunt, the Countess," said Emily, "that I am not going to marry until I am at least thirty years old!"

"Well, you will be quite on the shelf by that time, Emily. But perhaps Freddie will find you some elderly officer from the regiment who is looking for a bride?"

"Perhaps, but I hope that the war will be over by then, otherwise I might find myself a widow within a few months of marriage."

They then turned their conversation to more cheerful subjects, and the rest of the journey seemed to pass quite quickly. The carriage soon passed through the village of Marshfield and turned down the long slope on the hill into the city of Bath. Aunt Lucy's house was situated in the Paragon, just along the street from the Royal York Hotel. She gave both of them a very warm welcome.

"Julia! And this is your friend Emily Brandon? I'm so delighted to meet you, my dear. Have you had a pleasant journey? I have been looking forward so much to seeing you both, and have all kinds of plans for your entertainment."

Her butler collected the trunks from the carriage and arranged for the footman to take them upstairs. The house was on four levels, with the main entertaining rooms on the first floor stretching from the front to the back of the house, each beautifully furnished with silk curtains and handsome carpets.

Soon their trunks had been unpacked by the maids and they

were able to change from their dusty travelling clothes into fresh apparel.

Both Julia and Emily had bedrooms at the front of the house, overlooking the street, where there was a constant parade of fashionable people visible below, going to and from the Baths and the Assembly Rooms. However, they did not stay long looking at the view, as a delicious repast awaited them in the dining room below.

"How is your father, Julia? I know that your dear mama has been worried about him, and goodness knows he has had a few problems, one way and another, over the past two or three years."

"I am concerned about him, too, and the doctor does not seem to be able to do very much to improve the situation. I would have liked him to have come with me, but he seems to get tired so easily, and Mama said that the journey might be too much."

Aunt Lucy looked very concerned. "That's a great pity, for there are many expert medical men practising in Bath who might be able to help him."

Emily agreed with her. But the conversation turned to more cheerful subjects, and it was clear that Aunt Lucy did not intend Julia to have very much spare time in which to worry about her father.

There was to be a concert at the Lower Assembly Rooms tomorrow afternoon, and Aunt Lucy had purchased tickets for all three of them so that they could attend. She had in mind a little shopping in Milsom Street before that, interrupted perhaps by taking a few cakes in one of the tearooms during the morning. She had seen a very modish new dress in the window of one of the dressmakers, and wondered whether Julia would be interested in having that style made up from the length of silk that

Emily had purchased for her at Wilding and Kent's emporium in London.

"If you would like to read a little whilst you are staying with me, don't forget that there is a subscription library that you can use in Milsom Street. I recall that you are very fond of books."

"It sounds as though I may not have time for that, Aunt. I told Emily that you would make sure that we were very busy during our stay!"

Aunt Lucy smiled, and then said, "It's getting rather late now, so perhaps we should not wait too long before going to bed, so that you are fresh and ready to start everything tomorrow morning."

The following days were filled with a round of activities, with every waking moment occupied by making visits to Aunt Lucy's friends, listening to music at the concerts, visiting all the delightful shops, meeting acquaintances on the streets, and getting ready on many evenings to go to one of the balls.

"I am really quite exhausted," joked Julia, "and have met so many eligible young men that I cannot possibly remember all their names."

"Some of them are so good-looking that I might even decide to bring forward my plans for marriage from thirty to twenty," said Emily.

Aunt Lucy had done her best to make sure that they met every handsome young man worthy of consideration who was staying in Bath. Whilst there were many young ladies wearing the latest fashions, Aunt Lucy thought that Julia, and Emily also, of course, looked as well dressed as anyone at the concerts and balls.

Certainly, there was no shortage of the most fashionable young gentlemen with shapely calves and powerful thighs clad in breeches. Aunt Lucy was not immune to all that either, and wondered that her niece seemed to be so unimpressed by all the handsome young bucks to whom she had been introduced. Julia did not seem to find any of them interesting, but she could only do her best.

There was no news from Freddie, but Harriet wrote to say that Papa was taking life quietly by resting as much as he could, and that the doctor had called, with undisclosed results. Mr. Douglas had visited and his company had seemed to cheer their father. Sophie had been, as ever, irrepressible during his visit, so that Mama had to ask her to leave Papa with Mr. Douglas in peace.

"Sophie is always the same!" was Julia's response.

A few days later, a letter arrived for Aunt Lucy during breakfast. She undid the seal, unfolded the paper, and read slowly through the contents. Then her eyes began to fill with tears.

"Dear Aunt, whatever is the matter?"

"Oh Julia, this is such a sad message. My dear friend Susannah Hatton has died. I knew that she had been unwell some months ago, but had had no idea that it was so serious."

"I am so sorry, Aunt Lucy," said Julia. "Had you known each other a long time?"

"Yes, my dear, we had been at school together and kept in touch over all the years since then. So it seems that we have been friends forever."

"Does the letter say anything else?"

"Yes, it does. In her will, she has asked that several friends should choose something from her house at Morancourt, as a legacy that they would like to remember her by. That is a very kind idea, Julia, isn't it?"

"Yes, indeed. When are you planning to do that?"

"Her heir writes that he is to visit Bath soon, and plans to call on me so that we can make suitable arrangements."

"Do you know anything about him, Aunt?"

"Very little, Julia. All I can tell you is that he writes a good letter, and is keen to carry out my dear friend's wishes."

Aunt Lucy had been very insistent that the new dress should be made for Julia during her visit to Bath. Much time had been spent deciding on the design and having fittings to make sure that everything was exactly as it should be. Emily was delighted that her friend was to have that and several other new things. Julia was rather more cautious, for the new patterns were rather more flamboyant than she was used to, perhaps a bit more "London style" than she felt comfortable with.

However, Aunt Lucy was having none of it. "Blue is so becoming to your slim figure and delicate colouring, Julia. It would be such a pity if such an attractive girl as you were not to be shown to the best advantage."

Since Emily was of the same opinion, Julia did not argue any more, but agreed to select some simple jewellery, and other accessories, to complement her dress. Indeed, it seemed that Aunt Lucy had been right, since her new attire attracted many favourable comments, not only from the dowagers at the concerts and balls they attended, but also in the added attention she was receiving from all the beaux.

Julia and Emily heard no more about the legacy until the following week, when Aunt Lucy told them that a gentleman would be visiting her later that morning.

"Julia, my dear, be sure to wear one of the newer dresses that you brought with you from Derbyshire. Perhaps the yellow that is so becoming?"

Certainly, Julia did like the dress very much, and it seemed to be similar to the very latest fashion.

"What a pity," said Emily, "that I have arranged to visit the dressmaker today at ten thirty, for I would dearly have loved to meet him. However, Julia can tell me all about it."

As instructed, her friend took more care than usual in getting ready, with Martha, her aunt's maid, brushing her hair until the golden-brown lights in it shone. Julia suspected that all this effort might prove to be wasted, since their visitor might be an elderly man indifferent to the charms of a young lady. But her aunt had been so kind to her that she did not wish to be a disappointment.

Aunt Lucy and her niece were ready in the drawing room at the time agreed, and Julia walked across the room to look out of the window at the passing crowds. The visitor was a few minutes late, but just after eleven o'clock they heard the butler announcing his arrival.

"The Master of Morancourt, Mr. Christopher Hatton, ma'am."

"You are very welcome, sir," said her aunt.

"Thank you, you are most kind, Mrs. Harrison."

Julia heard his voice, turned, and looked at him with amazement. For there in the doorway, regarding her with an astonishment equal to her own, was Kit Douglas.

FIVE

"May I introduce my niece, my sister's eldest daughter, Miss Maitland?"

Her aunt did not appear to notice Julia's confusion.

"Miss Maitland, I am delighted to make your acquaintance," said the Master of Morancourt, bowing to Julia.

She did not know what to think. Did Kit Douglas want her aunt to believe that they were meeting for the first time? For the moment, it seemed best not to challenge this.

"Sir," was all she said, curtseying to him.

He turned back towards Aunt Lucy.

"As you know, Mrs. Harrison, I am here to discuss Mrs. Hatton's legacy. My godmother often mentioned you very warmly to me, and I know that you had had a very lengthy acquaintance—since your school days, I believe?"

"Please sit down, Mr. Hatton." She gestured towards a chair and waited until he was seated before replying.

"Yes, that's true; she was probably the friend that I had known for the longest. I'm very sorry that I did not know of her serious illness, for I would have liked to visit her."

"I was there for the last week before she died," he said, "but she was aware of very little for most of that time."

She nodded and then pulled the bell cord. When he came

into the room, Aunt Lucy asked the butler to bring some re-freshments. Just as this was being arranged, they could hear the footman answering the door. The butler soon returned, looking rather flustered.

"Ma'am, there is a messenger at the door for you. I apologise for the interruption, but it might be easier if you could come and speak to him yourself."

Aunt Lucy looked puzzled, but rose from her seat and, excusing herself, followed him out of the room.

Kit Douglas turned immediately to Julia.

"Miss Maitland, you must be surprised by the manner of my greeting to you?"

"Yes, sir." She hesitated, then said, "Please explain."

"I had a letter from my father last week. He passed on the news that you had gone away so that you could enjoy a change of scene and forget for a while all about your parents' plans for you in Derbyshire. I had no idea that you were related to Mrs. Harrison, or that you were staying with her."

"There is no reason why you should have done, Mr. Douglas."

"My immediate reaction therefore on seeing you here was that you would prefer not to be reminded about Derbyshire at present, or for your aunt to know of our previous acquaintance."

Julia smoothed her hands down the skirt of her dress, then again, then she composed herself and clasped her hands together in front of her with the appearance of calm, although her mind was racing. No one she had met in Bath had mentioned his family or Norton Place to her, and Emily had not met Kit Douglas, although she had heard of him.

Kit Douglas was looking at her intently. "You have reservations? I will do as you wish, of course."

Julia paused. Perhaps a question could resolve her dilemma.

"Have you met many people of your own acquaintance here in Bath, sir?"

"No. On my visits to my godmother after the death of her husband, Mr. Henry Hatton, I had only passed through the city and not stopped here. And now, one of the requirements of my godmother's will was that I should change my surname to hers. She had no children, you see. You will know that it is quite common with the bequest of an estate for the heir to be asked to assume the family name."

Julia smiled to herself—a new name! Would she be able to remember that?

She could not realise what effect her infectious smile was having on him. He waited, regarding her gravely, admiring her neat figure, the way that her hair curled at the nape of her neck, and her clear grey eyes.

"How long will you be staying in Bath, sir?"

Suddenly, he smiled at her in return. "That depends, I suppose, on the company that I might keep, and what else I might find to do. Are you planning to be here with your aunt for long?"

Julia's mood rapidly sobered.

"I don't know. I am anxious for any news that comes about my father from Derbyshire. I am very concerned for his health, and only came to visit Aunt Lucy because he insisted that I should."

They heard in the distance that the voices in discussion at the front door had ceased, and her aunt came back into the drawing room.

"Please excuse me, Mr. Hatton, for that unfortunate diversion—only a domestic matter. I really do think that my butler could have dealt with it himself. However, now, where were we?"

"I suppose that we were about to discuss how and when you might visit my godmother's home to choose your gift. You will recall that Morancourt is more than a day's drive from here. I have kept on her servants at the property, and I should be delighted to offer you hospitality for as long as you might wish to stay."

"That is most generous of you, sir. I have my own travelling chaise, so I could use that for the journey. But at present I have Julia staying with me, and her friend Emily also. Julia was to return to Derbyshire with her. Do you have a particular date in mind?"

Julia could see that Kit Douglas—no, she should think of him as Mr. Hatton—was considering the options. Before he could speak, her aunt continued.

"Of course, sir, Julia could accompany me if you did not object to that."

Julia said nothing, but he read her expression accurately.

"Miss Maitland may prefer to continue in Bath. I cannot offer her any comparable social delights at Morancourt, delighted though I would be if she were to visit."

She was grateful for his thoughtfulness, and amused at the different levels on which his words were being received by her aunt and by herself.

Aunt Lucy, unaware of this, clearly considered that a visit to Dorset would be a pleasant diversion for her niece. She looked to Julia, but could see that for some reason she was not keen to accept the invitation.

"Let me leave you now, ma'am, and I can return when you have considered the matter further. There is no particular urgency, from my point of view, to have a decision now."

The subject was pursued no longer and, after a few more minutes of easy conversation, he left.

"What a most agreeable young man, Julia. So cultured and with such a stylish manner—so superior to some of the young men you will have met in Bath. I do appreciate that it was your intention just to visit me here, but a few days away in Dorset might be very pleasant as a change of scene."

"I came to Bath to visit you, dear aunt, not to endure another long journey and spend my time in a dusty old house with someone I don't know."

Her aunt made a face but decided not to argue, and the matter was left until Emily came back from the dressmakers. Then Aunt Lucy told her all about the visit from the Master of Morancourt, how handsome he was, how pleasant, and about the suggested visit.

Emily could see that Julia did not agree with her aunt about travelling to Dorset, but it was not until later, when they were alone, that she asked her friend what the problem was.

By this time, Julia had had the opportunity to decide on her reply.

"He was pleasant, certainly, but I don't want to go down to Dorset when I could be here with you, enjoying the delights of Bath, which is what I came to do."

"Very well, let us be as gay as we may, for certainly life back in Derbyshire will not be so interesting or as lively when we return there."

Over the next days, the two young ladies made the most of the social activities available in Bath. They took the waters in the Pump Room and met friends for tea at both the Upper and Lower Assembly Rooms. Accompanied by Aunt Lucy, they attended a concert on the Monday and a dress ball on the

Thursday evening, where they met several young gentlemen who had arrived just that week in the city.

One of these, Patrick Jepson, had been introduced to them by the master of ceremonies earlier in the evening, and he came across the room to speak to Aunt Lucy. The tails of his long dress coat fell well below the backs of his knees, and the padding on the shoulders of his coat jacket was so exaggerated that it rivalled the height of his intricately folded neck cloth. He had prominent and unusually shaped ears, and his hair was curled and overdressed in the latest style. The view of this apparition caused Emily to giggle behind her hand and Julia to turn briefly away towards the wall to compose herself.

Mr. Jepson inquired of Emily, "Miss Brandon, do you come from the family living at Cressborough Castle in Derbyshire?"

Julia observed with amusement Emily's cautious reply, asking the reason for his question.

"Well, in that case I know your brother Dominic, he's a friend of mine in town."

He can't know the family very well, Julia thought.

"Dominic is my cousin, Mr. Jepson, not my brother. How do you know him?"

"We go around together in London with some other fellows, visiting the clubs, playing cards, going to the races—things like that."

Emily said nothing, but he went on. "Would you do me the honour of the next dance, Miss Brandon?" he said, looking at Aunt Lucy as he did so.

She nodded imperceptibly at Emily, who gave Julia a private smile before she inclined her head briefly to Mr. Jepson and allowed herself to be led onto the dance floor.

"I don't like that young man," said Julia.

"No, I agree, but Emily is well able to take care of herself with us nearby." Then she pointed across the room. "Why look, Julia, there is Mr. Hatton."

She turned and saw across the room that Kit Douglas—no, she must remember to say Mr. Hatton—was looking towards her with a small smile, and then making his way around the edge of the dancers in the centre of the room to reach them.

"Mrs. Harrison, Miss Maitland, I was beginning to think that there was no really pleasant company here this evening!"

"That is a little harsh, sir."

"Maybe, ma'am, but you must agree that there are some very gaudy coxcombs on the floor, and some very overdressed young ladies."

Julia could not conceal an involuntary laugh at her aunt's expression.

Mr. Hatton himself was wearing a well-cut jacket in the latest fashion, with a neatly tied neck cloth matching his shirt. His long cream pantaloons above the mirror shine of his shoes made him look even taller than he was. His dark hair was properly dressed, but without the extremity of style exhibited by some of the other young blades in the room.

"Miss Maitland, if your aunt will permit it, will you do me the honour of dancing the next?"

Julia did not need to look at Aunt Lucy. "I should be delighted, Mr. Hatton."

As they stood at the side of the room waiting for the dance to finish in the centre of the floor, Mr. Hatton said, "Have you heard of the continental dance—the waltz—Miss Maitland? I was introduced to it whilst I was in Spain last year."

"I have heard only," Julia smiled, "that the dowagers do not approve of it, for I understand that the couples dance very close together and almost in an embrace, and that the older ladies, and some mothers, do not agree with that?"

"Yes, that is true, but I have seen the dance myself, and the waltz is a most graceful spectacle if done well. I took a few lessons whilst I was in Spain and, now that my leg is mending, I should love to try the waltz again."

"I have heard," Julia said, "that the dance has been introduced in Almack's in London. If that is so, perhaps we provincials may be allowed to try it out soon."

He laughed as he replied, "True, it takes time for those of us who live outside town to learn new habits. But now that I have a ballroom of my own—"

"A ballroom! You must have a very large house in Dorset, sir?"

"No—not very large, but the wife of the gentleman who built the manor at Morancourt was very fond of dancing—so the house has a modest-sized ballroom."

But then, before they could continue their conversation, it was time for them to take their places for the next dance.

Once they were out of earshot of others, he said, "Miss Maitland, I had been hoping to have the chance to speak with you privately before I visit your aunt's house again. I know that you have doubts about making the journey to Dorset. I certainly do not wish you to think that I am trying to dictate what you should do."

His words brought to mind his conversation at Norton Place a few weeks earlier.

"We share that view, sir, I believe."

"Yes. But I would very much value your opinion if you were to be willing to come with her. The estate at Morancourt has been allowed to run down considerably. My godmother was very wealthy, and money was not a problem. But she did not have the energy in her last years to take any interest in renovating the house or the grounds. But now that I find myself in charge, and able to afford to do as I like, there are many things that I would like to alter. But I have had no experience in taking such a property in hand."

Julia looked at him blankly, for he must know that she had no such experience either. It must be, therefore, that he sought to have her company, and that her aunt's visit would be a good excuse for achieving that.

"Aunt Lucy has good taste, so I'm sure that she would be willing to help you."

He looked at her warily, not sure whether that was intended to be a firm negative.

They continued in the dance for several minutes until the music came to an end.

Then he said, "I should be honest with you, Miss Maitland. I would particularly like you to assist me. It is very important to me that you should."

As he spoke, they had been walking across the room towards the refreshments, and now they came upon Aunt Lucy and Emily, who were looking for Julia.

Before Julia could answer him, Emily interrupted.

"I had a very odd conversation during the dance with Mr. Jepson, Julia. He said that Dominic has been down here in Bath, and travelling in the West Country and further south near the coast on some kind of business venture. What kind of venture could that be? I don't recall Freddie saying anything about it."

"Well, there may be no truth in it or, more likely, Dominic doesn't tell Freddie everything. Indeed, that may be just as well." And she introduced her friend to Mr. Hatton.

Mr. Hatton gave a discreet cough. "Perhaps these are private family matters, Miss Brandon. If you will excuse me, I will go and fetch a glass of cordial for Miss Maitland, and some for you and Mrs. Harrison also, if I may."

When he returned, he handed the glasses of cordial to the ladies, and then addressed Aunt Lucy.

"Mrs. Harrison, you have lived in Bath for many years, I believe? Now that the new canal is open between Bath and Reading, journeys by boat are being offered from the canal junction with the River Avon here in the city to the rear entrance to the Sydney Pleasure Gardens. Would you allow me to escort you and these two young ladies on such an expedition—perhaps later this week?"

"Mr. Hatton, that is most kind. I have been to the Sydney Gardens many times over the years, of course. I am not personally anxious to make a journey on the canal, but I am sure that Julia and Emily would be very delighted to accept your invitation. Is that not so, my dears?"

Emily clapped her hands together with glee, and Julia replied for them both.

"Mr. Hatton, that would an expedition that we could never have the opportunity to enjoy at home. I have not been on a canal, and I have heard a great deal about the Sydney Gardens. We really enjoyed our trip last month to the Vauxhall Gardens with Emily's cousin."

"Oh, I did not realise that Lord Brandon had taken you there?" He suddenly appeared very downcast.

"Not Dominic Brandon, we did not meet him in London. It was Freddie, his younger brother, who took time out from his regiment to take us to Vauxhall. That is a very much larger and busier place. I am sure that Sydney Gardens will be very different, but just as enjoyable."

Mr. Hatton's mood seemed to lift as quickly as it had fallen, and the arrangements were made for him to call at Aunt Lucy's house later in the week to walk with them to the beginning of the canal. He continued his conversation with Julia's aunt for a few more minutes before excusing himself.

Aunt Lucy watched him go, and then turned to Emily.

"I do not know your cousins, but I do think that it might be better if you were more discreet in discussing matters concerning them in front of strangers."

"Mr. Hatton isn't really a stranger to you, Mrs. Harrison, and anyway, it's his own fault if Dominic chooses friends who go round telling anybody and everybody what he is getting up to!"

To prevent an argument developing with her guest, Aunt Lucy changed the subject quickly, and no further private discussion took place that evening.

⚜

The boat was full of excited passengers as Mr. Hatton and the young ladies set off on the boat to go through the canal locks at Widcombe. To begin with, they stood together on the stern, but then Emily walked towards the front of the vessel and fell into conversation with a party who was visiting from London.

Julia stood in companionable silence with Mr. Hatton as the horses on the towpath pulled the boat past the rear gardens of tall houses in golden stone on the eastern side of the canal and the view towards Bath Abbey and the centre of the city to the west. As she watched the houses go by, it seemed to Julia that at last there was an opportunity for her to find out what she so much wanted to know.

"Might I ask you a question, Mr. Hatton?"

He turned towards her and nodded, his eyes alert.

"The red shoes—why did you give them to me?"

There was a long pause before he answered her.

"At the time, I hardly knew. It was almost involuntary. And I need not have delivered them in person, of course. But I have had plenty of time since then to think about it, to remember your visit to Norton Place, and you, Miss Maitland."

There was so much in his green eyes that spoke to her as he continued.

"Only since then have I been able to be honest with myself. I wanted to see your home at Banford Hall and to let you have something very personal to me. I had heard that your parents, perhaps in particular your mother, want you to marry someone quite above my social circle—Lord Brandon, perhaps—and I knew that I might never see you again."

Her grey eyes looked at him without wavering for a moment. Then she said, "Men have more freedom than women in such matters, Mr. Hatton, as I have been finding to my cost."

"True, but I will always be the younger son of a self-made man who made his fortune in trade. The fact that my mother was the daughter of a baronet does not seem to compensate for that."

"But your father made his fortune by his own efforts—surely many people would say that is praiseworthy?"

"Maybe, but not enough to make me or my brother respectable in the highest circles, removed as we are only one generation from a grandfather who was a small farmer."

She looked out over the side of the boat, then back to face him.

"I appreciated your gift very much, Mr. Hatton, then and now, and I'm very happy to be able to thank you. I should have done so before. As to the future, so much depends on my father's health. The doctor has told us that he has serious problems with his heart, and that there is little that can be done. As long as he lives, I should not be forced to marry someone I dislike or despise. But if anything happens to him, my mother might have very different priorities."

"There must be an expert physician here who could help him? Or someone from London? Sir William Knighton treated my godmother successfully in Bath for her heart affliction for several years with a carefully measured dosage of digitalis, made from the leaves of the foxglove plant. He is very well recommended."

"Bath and London are a long way from Derbyshire, Mr. Hatton. Papa is not well enough to travel any distance, and the cost of taking a doctor to him would be very considerable, even if that could be arranged."

"Do you have the red shoes with you?"

"No, sir." She saw his expression change and he turned his head away. Almost without knowing why, she added, "I could not risk losing them."

The change in his face was wonderful to see as he looked back at Julia, and he was about to reply when Emily returned, saying that they were approaching the lock on the canal. She stood between Mr. Hatton and Julia as they watched with careful attention the raising of the water and the boat in the confined space of the lock up to the next level of the canal.

"You are interested in how things work, Miss Brandon?" he said. "It seems a very elegant solution to moving the boat around the contours of the hill, and that presumably means less work in digging the canal."

"Julia would be more anxious than I to know the exact details, Mr. Hatton," said Emily, smiling at her friend.

"Yes. It's true that I am more interested in how problems can be solved, Mr. Hatton. So was my brother, for he told me that, without change, there can be no progress."

He laughed. "Yes, that is very true, although not everyone would agree with you, Miss Maitland. And the next change lies ahead of us, for now we can see the Chinese bridge ahead."

"Was that made of iron in the foundry at Coalbrookdale started by Abraham Darby? My father has told me about the factory there."

"Yes, as well as the second and wider iron bridge beyond. And can you see the entrance to Sydney Gardens coming into sight between them, on the left?"

Once disembarked at the Gardens, the three young people followed the other groups of visitors around the gravel walk. Music was being provided by the Pandean Band—several exotically dressed musicians playing pan pipes together with percussion instruments, making sounds the likes of which Emily and Julia had never heard before.

On the other side of the path, there was a sign advertising the new Cascade, with water making a tinkling noise, and appearing to rush down a village street.

"That is powered by clockwork and, if you look closely, the 'water' is really moving bits of tin plate."

"You are very knowledgeable, sir," said Emily, impressed.

"Perhaps, Mr. Hatton, you might have read about it in this week's edition of the *Bath Chronicle*," said Julia, laughing at their host, and he had to acknowledge that she was right.

"It is very difficult to gain much personal credit with either of you ladies around, Miss Brandon! But let me divert you, for I understand that there is to be a balloon ascent in a few minutes at the other end of the Gardens."

Julia and Emily walked across the gravel with Mr. Hatton,

watching with amazement as the aeronaut lit the fire under the canopy and his passenger looked on as the assistants released the ropes securing the basket below to the ground. Then the balloon rose steadily above the upturned faces of the crowd as the fire roared, and it was blown southwards away from them above the city. Afterwards, they walked back together towards Pulteney Bridge and the centre of Bath, enjoying the view in each direction after they had crossed the river.

Aunt Lucy was highly entertained by their account of these events at the breakfast table on the next day, but refused to promise that she would take a canal trip herself, although they assured her that she would not feel seasick.

Over the next few days, Emily continued to encourage Julia to accept Mr. Hatton's invitation to accompany her aunt.

"You have never been to Dorset, and I am told that it is very beautiful and quite different from Derbyshire. Why don't you go? Your aunt would be delighted to have your company. I won't be able to stay here much longer now that I need to go back to London, as I have had a letter to say that my aunt and uncle will be arriving at their town house soon."

Julia promised to think carefully about what she should do. In fact, she realised now, she knew exactly what she wanted and, for once, she could not think of any reason why she should make a different decision.

The day came when the Master of Morancourt kept his appointment to visit Aunt Lucy. She had not pressed Julia any further, and so it was with some curiosity that she waited to hear what her niece's reply would be.

Mr. Hatton repeated what he had said to Julia in private in the Assembly Rooms, that he would value her opinion on what he should do at Morancourt.

"Very well, sir, since you are so very persuasive, and Aunt Lucy has made it clear that she would like to have my company during her visit. My only proviso must be that, if I have any message about my father's health, I might need to cut short my stay to return to Derbyshire."

Aunt Lucy was delighted at this news, and smiled at Emily, who was sitting quietly in a chair on the other side of the room.

Julia was more interested in Mr. Hatton's reaction, but that was only confirmed as he left. He took her hand in farewell and, as he did so, he whispered, "I shall be so delighted to have your company, Miss Maitland. Thank you."

He was escorted from the room by her aunt and, as soon as they had left, Emily said, "Bravo, Julia, well done. I haven't dared say so before, but he is quite the most agreeable young man that we have met during our stay here. But how will you return home, Julia, if you do not travel with me?"

"Aunt Lucy has said that she will take me home to Derbyshire herself. It is some time since she visited my parents, and so she has very kindly said that she will bring forward her next visit to the north."

Julia could have added that she suspected Aunt Lucy of some curiosity to meet the heir to an earldom that Julia's mama had in mind as a suitor for her niece, although they had had very little discussion about it.

However, her friend then changed the subject to quite a different matter.

"Do you remember, Julia, when we met Mr. Hatton at the Assembly Rooms, that I told you about my conversation with Mr. Jepson. But I didn't tell you about everything that was said."

Julia looked at her curiously.

"He said that Dominic is very short of money. That is despite the very generous allowance I know he gets every month from my uncle and aunt. If that's the case, he must be spending a very great deal on Christina, or other young women, or on gaming, or must have very large debts of some other kind."

"Well, Emily, that's not unusual for young men of quality—they seem to think that it's fashionable to waste as much money as they can in as short a time as possible."

"Maybe, but why would he make a journey down to this part of the country, and what kind of venture would he get involved in? As far as I know, he has no business experience of any kind. After he left Oxford, he served for two years in the regiment, but he has done nothing else that I'm aware of."

"Well, all we can hope for is that most of his friends are more sensible, and less stupidly dressed, than Mr. Jepson, not to mention those unusual ears."

"I do wish that I thought you were right, Julia."

That evening as she fell asleep, she thought to herself what a difficult situation she would find herself in if she agreed to marry Dominic Brandon. However keen Mama might be on the match, Julia didn't want to believe that she would insist that her daughter's future should be in the hands of someone who seemed likely to be unfaithful, profligate, and, by the sound of it, not very good at anything except spending money.

The next day Julia wrote to her parents to advise them of the change of plan, saying that Mr. Hatton, as the new owner of Morancourt, was going to be their host for several days. She doubted whether either Papa or Mama would be worried about the idea, but Aunt Lucy had advised her that they ought to know of it. Only a few days now remained before they were planning to go to Dorset.

"Mr. Hatton has told me that he is leaving for Morancourt

tomorrow, Julia. I have invited him to dine with us tonight, I hope that you don't object."

"No, of course not, Aunt. And it will be a pleasant way of saying good-bye to Emily, too."

The two young ladies asked that Aunt Lucy's dresser, Martha Fisher, should help them both with their toilette for the evening. She was a local girl who had been working in the house for several years as a maid before Aunt Lucy had decided to promote her to a more responsible position, looking after her mistress and her clothes.

"If you please, Miss Julia," Martha said, "my mistress suggested that you might like to borrow her sapphire necklace to go with your new dress? And for Miss Emily, there are several other jewels that you might like to choose from."

"How very generous of Mrs. Harrison, and thank you, Martha. Perhaps you could bring the box to me so that I can choose something to go with the grey dress that I brought with me from the castle."

It took the two young ladies nearly an hour to complete their toilette and all the details, but Aunt Lucy's pleasure in their appearance when they arrived in the drawing room made it all worthwhile.

Mr. Hatton arrived at the appointed time, looking immaculate in his evening dress, and bearing a small gift for his hostess that was beautifully wrapped in silver coloured paper tied with a red ribbon.

"You are very generous, sir. Please take a seat. We shall be dining in about half an hour. In the meantime, perhaps you would be kind enough to tell us all a little more about Morancourt, for neither of the young ladies has been there."

"Well, ma'am, I am a biased observer, but I will do my best.

The house itself is looking tired and much in need of redecoration and new furnishings. You may remember that it is neither too small nor too large but, towards the end of her life, my godmother only lived in two rooms on the ground floor because of her heart condition. Her servants cared for her very well, in particular the housekeeper, Mrs. Jones. Her husband has been looking after the grounds around the house for my godmother, but had been given no instructions to do anything apart from keeping the grass cut with the help of the gardeners. Mr. Whitaker is a younger man who has been in charge of the farm stock and the rest of the land, which is generally in good condition, although there is a need for investment in new buildings."

"How much land is there, Mr. Hatton?" asked Emily.

"About five hundred acres, Miss Brandon, plus the park immediately around the house, which has an area of about forty acres. Mrs. Harrison will remember that the manor house is about five miles from the sea, on one side of the Marshwood Vale, which is a very attractive rural area between Lyme Regis and Dorchester. I believe that you have not been in Dorset yourself, Miss Brandon?"

"No, although I am beginning to wish that I may have the opportunity sometime in the future."

"I think you said, Mr. Hatton," said Julia, "that your godmother was a widow with no children?"

"Yes, her husband, Henry, was given the house many years ago by an uncle who had been one of a large family. You can see that, in some of the bedrooms, the children's toys are still stored in cupboards, as though they might come back at any time. When I visited the house with my mother as a child I used to play with some of them."

Aunt Lucy was obviously charmed by this idea, but at that

moment the butler entered the drawing room to announce that dinner was served. The rest of the evening passed with pleasant conversation before their guest took his leave.

The following day was Wednesday, the last day that the young ladies would have together before Emily had to leave for London. The Brandon's carriage arrived early in the morning from town with Annette Labonne, the Countess's maid. After luncheon, she was to pack Emily's clothes for the journey back to London the next day.

Julia and Emily went out in the sunshine and spent most of the morning shopping in Milsom Street, where they paused at Mollands' pastry shop for a few minutes to take tea and cakes. They were seated at a table inside the window, watching the crowds pass by, when Emily suddenly exclaimed to her friend, "Look, Julia, isn't that Dominic on the other side of the road?"

They both peered through the glass and, between the various people passing by, saw that it was indeed Dominic Brandon, talking to Mr. Jepson.

"I wonder if Mr. Jepson will tell him that I'm here?" Emily leant back in her chair. "I don't really want to know what Dominic is up to."

"Nor I. We will not make ourselves known to him, for I am sure that I do not want to meet Dominic myself," said Julia.

At that moment, they were amazed to see Annette Labonne approaching the two gentlemen along the pavement and, when they met, Dominic and his friend were clearly not surprised to see her. For several minutes, the three were engaged in deep conversation, oblivious to their surroundings and the two young ladies watching from the shop across the street.

At last Dominic and Mr. Jepson doffed their hats to Annette, and she walked quickly away in the direction of Aunt Lucy's house. Emily and Julia looked on as the two young men then turned away and proceeded together down the road towards the Abbey.

"How extraordinary," said Julia at last. "What can they have been discussing?"

"I have no idea, but I won't say anything about it to her at present, or to the Countess when I see her in town. But nor will I forget, for Dominic and Mr. Jepson were not surprised to see Annette and must have arranged to meet her there. Something very odd is going on."

"Well, Mr. Jepson was right about your cousin Dominic visiting the city. When Freddie is next on leave, Emily, try to speak to him about it. And please don't tell my aunt anything."

"Of course not."

"I hope that I don't see Dominic again whilst I'm here. I really do not want to think about anything to do with Derbyshire whilst I'm here in Bath."

As soon as she had spoken, Julia realised that there was an exception to that. Mr. Hatton might not have been part of her life in Derbyshire, but Kit Douglas certainly had been.

SIX

The next day, the friends said an emotional farewell to each other and promised to meet again as soon as Julia had returned to Derbyshire. Emily had a large number of new purchases to accommodate in the outside box at the back of the Brandon family's carriage, as well as inside next to Annette Labonne, and she also took with her some gifts that Julia had purchased for her younger sisters.

At her aunt's suggestion, Julia rested after luncheon before they set to work to pack their trunks for their journey.

Aunt Lucy spent the next two hours choosing and then changing the clothes that they would take with them to Dorset. "We may not find ourselves in fine company, Julia, but it is possible that we should be invited to some social events whilst we are staying with Mr. Hatton. So make sure, my dear, that you have at least two of your best dresses with you. I will send Martha now to help you, so that we are ready to leave in the morning soon after breakfast. She can do my trunk after yours."

The weather proved to be rather grey as they left Bath the next day. It had rained during the night, and the carriage wheels kept slipping on the cobbled surface as the horses pulled the carriage towards the bridge over the River Avon. Julia gazed wide-eyed at the poorly dressed people at this end of the city, for she had heard that it was the rougher part of town, and Aunt Lucy had warned her not to venture there on her own.

"You see what I meant, Julia?"

She did indeed, although to assume that everyone who was rather poorly dressed must be unpleasant or threatening seemed to Julia to be going rather too far.

"Have you ever come to this end of Bath, Martha?" asked Julia.

"Yes, Miss, but never on my own, and only during the day time. I would not risk it at night, for I have heard some terrible tales of robbery."

"And worse," said Aunt Lucy.

The locality did not seem much improved on the other side of the river, as the carriage passed by the mean houses huddled together along the street, and was pulled by the horses up the Holloway Hill on the far side of the city.

However, once beyond the edge of Bath, the dilapidated yellow stone houses gave way to open green fields as they made their way along the Wells Road and on through pleasant countryside and then down the slope into Norton Radstock. There they stopped to rest the horses for a few minutes at the coaching inn.

Whilst they waited, Martha ventured to say that her elder brother Jem had worked in the town.

"What does he do?" asked Julia.

"He is a coal miner, Miss. There has been mining in the area in Somerset, especially around Radstock, for a long time. Those strange pointed hills that you can see over there are not natural; they are made from the coal waste."

Julia was surprised, for she had not realised that there was any mining in Somerset. She looked at the conical shapes with interest, for she was familiar with coal mining near Derby, for fluorspar for decorative objects and iron smelting on the Brandons' land near Cressborough Castle, and in the lead mines on other estates nearby in Derbyshire.

"Is your brother working here now, Martha?"

"No, Miss, he has got a new job with some of the other men. They are busy down by the coast. But I don't know exactly where. He only comes back home every month or so. But my mother says that he's getting good money."

Aunt Lucy looked at her maid with surprise, then at Julia, raising her eyebrows in disbelief. But she didn't say anything until they stopped for the night at an inn near Yeovil, and she came into Julia's bedchamber to make sure that she was comfortable for the night.

"Martha must have got that wrong, Julia, about her brother, I mean, for I don't know of any mining taking place down near the coast. She's a nice girl, but not always very bright."

Sometimes her aunt could be rather dogmatic, thought Julia, just like Mama. Martha seemed to her to be as bright as anyone in her aunt's employment.

The following morning, the weather seemed better and the carriage made good progress past Yeovil and towards Halstock. The colour of the local stone in the buildings now was tinged with brown amongst the yellow, and most of the roofs were thatched, although many were in a state of disrepair. The tumbled green fields were so small that Julia thought that they must be quite difficult to farm, but the wild hedgerows seemed to be full of singing birds as they passed by, with some of the branches almost meeting across the narrow lanes above the top of the carriage.

Julia had brought a book with her for the journey, but trying to read as the carriage shook from side to side on the rough surface was almost impossible. Aunt Lucy dozed fitfully opposite her. Martha gripped the seat rather tightly with her hands, and just managed to smile at Julia.

"I was interested in what you mentioned yesterday about your brother, Martha. Did you say he was down here, mining near the coast?"

"I didn't say mining, Miss, for I don't know exactly what Jem's doing. Only that he and some of his mates were offered work with very good pay at the end of last year, and he's been down there ever since. I haven't seen him on any of my days off since then."

"Do you have any other family, Martha?"

"Yes, Miss. My widowed mother still lives in Radstock with the younger children, but my elder sister is married. She and her husband have a cottage in a village near Gloucester, to the north-west near the River Severn. And one of my younger brothers is working in a woollen mill, and he lives with an aunt in Trowbridge, a few miles to the east of Bath."

The carriage stopped to rest the horses for a few minutes at the Fox Inn, hidden in the green valley at Corscombe, before making its way up the narrow lane beyond to reach the crossroads with the main route from the county town of Dorchester at the top of the hill. Once safely across, they continued for about a mile across Beaminster Down. Then the coachman asked them to alight and walk behind the carriage for the next mile to lighten the load, as he held back the horses and drove with great care down the long steep slope. At the foot of the hill, they took their seats again and the carriage continued on a little further before they reached the centre of the small stone-built town of Beaminster. There, the carriage paused opposite the stone cross that indicated the location for the market. All around the centre of the little town square, honey-coloured hamstone houses with thatched roofs and shop fronts at ground-floor level were crowded together side by side with several inns, and all was bustle and activity in the market as the local people went about their business.

"Not far to go now, Miss," confided Martha, who had seen the directions to Morancourt given by Mr. Hatton, "only about three miles."

"Over there on the right is the Greyhound Inn, behind the market cross, Julia," said Aunt Lucy. "I will ask the coachman to fetch us all a glass of cordial. My throat is very parched."

The cool liquid was very welcome and, as soon as the tray and the glasses had been returned to the inn, the carriage set off on its way out of the square on the last stage of their journey.

Once they had left the edge of the town, the carriage plunged into yet another lane deeply set between the field boundaries on each side. Passing only the occasional cottage alongside the track, the surface was uneven and the route twisted and turned, up and down, until at last the wheels came to a stop. Julia looked out of the carriage window to see two tall old stone pillars framing a pair of worn wooden gates, with a thatched cottage on one side. The coachman got down from his perch and walked forwards to speak to someone standing by the gates, and slowly they were opened to let the carriage through.

To her surprise, they stopped on the far side, and a familiar voice could be heard speaking to the coachman. Then Mr. Hatton walked across to the carriage window.

"Mrs. Harrison, Miss Maitland, welcome to Morancourt! You have made very good time today," He smiled at Julia through the window. "I will ride ahead now, but you will see the manor house on the left as you go down the drive."

She could hear the clatter of the stirrups as he mounted his horse, and the sound of the hooves on the gravel, before the carriage lurched again into motion along the drive.

After a short interval, they negotiated a bend and there beyond was the house set back behind a rough lawn. On one side, the steep roof was thatched over old stone gables, with the walls pierced by wide mullioned timber windows at ground- and upper-floor levels. On the other side, in a wing three storeys' high of more recent date, the stone lintols were intricately carved over tall windows set into deep reveals in the walls above wide stone sills. The front door was set in a porch between the two wings, with a worn stone coat of arms just visible above the entrance. The low garden walls on each side of the house were almost invisible, buried in a tangle of flowers and shrubs. Behind them, there were glimpses of parkland through trellis arches and a fence woven from tree branches.

Once the carriage had stopped moving, Aunt Lucy eased herself with relief up from her seat and, helped by a footman, descended rather unsteadily down the carriage steps. Julia, followed by Martha, joined her at the front door, where Mr. Hatton was waiting for them with another footman standing beside him.

"Please come in, ladies," he said. He showed his guests into the hall, where the staff was lined up to greet them. He introduced the first as Mrs. Jones, his godmother's housekeeper, who asked one of the footmen to take their trunks upstairs. Then she led Aunt Lucy and Julia into the drawing room, where refreshments awaited them. Her aunt settled herself into a comfortable chair and engaged the housekeeper in conversation.

Meanwhile, Julia sat beside Mr. Hatton on the settee, and she took the opportunity to look around her. The drawing room was spacious and well lit, with carefully polished furniture against the walls and rather faded curtains at the windows. Every table and bookcase was covered with items of china and silverware, as well as other ornaments, many with elaborate detail and highly coloured.

"Your godmother collected ornamental items, Mr. Hatton?" she said.

"Yes. As you can see, there is no shortage of such objects, either here or in any of the other living rooms. I'm not sure that much of it is to my taste, but perhaps that is the difference between the generations. Do you think that your aunt will see anything that she would like?"

"Well, her taste is not the same as mine, either, but I'm sure that for sentimental reasons she will be able to choose something to remember your godmother by. Are there any items that you yourself will want to retain?"

"No. I will not decide whether to keep anything until her friends have chosen what they want. Then I will make up my mind whether I like what remains. I suppose it depends to some extent on how I will redecorate and furnish the house."

"Is this room typical of the condition elsewhere?"

"No—it is rather better than many of the other rooms. That is because in her last years my godmother lived only in this room and the salon adjoining, as she could not manage the stairs. Mrs. Jones made sure that these two rooms were well kept."

By this time Aunt Lucy had finished her refreshments, and Mr. Hatton invited them both to walk with him through the rest of the ground floor. As he had told Julia, some of the rooms were badly in need of attention. She asked her host if she might see the kitchen. Mrs. Jones, who was accompanying them, looked embarrassed, but Mr. Hatton said, "Yes, Miss Maitland, of course. I'm sure that you will understand that Mrs. Jones has done her best under rather difficult circumstances."

Mrs. Jones still looked reluctant, but led the way down a narrow passageway to the kitchen and pantry, which, although clean and tidy, were badly in need of renovation and redecoration. There seemed to be a shortage of storage space and the floor looked to be in need of attention. Mrs. Jones seemed to be very relieved when she was able to usher them back towards the entrance hall. There, she suggested that the ladies might like to go to their rooms to refresh themselves and to supervise the unpacking of their trunks. Aunt Lucy and Julia were happy to go along with this suggestion.

The two bedrooms, side by side, faced over the rear garden, with views for some distance up a long grassy expanse towards a ridge on the hill beyond. Aunt Lucy was disappointed not to find toys in the cupboard in her room, but Julia pointed out that the nurseries were most likely to be on the top floor above them.

Julia's room was furnished with elegant if outdated furniture of the character appropriate for a lady's boudoir. The drapes around the bed were a faded pink brocade hung on a mahogany frame. On the walls were several pictures, including one of a very handsome lady whom Julia guessed might be the late Mrs. Hatton. There were several ornamental items on a mahogany chest in the corner of the room, and a matching mahogany wardrobe beside it.

Martha had unpacked the trunk and was hanging the clothes in the wardrobe. After changing her dress, Julia went along the corridor to find Aunt Lucy and they descended the stairs together to the dining room. There they enjoyed a pleasant meal in the company of Mr. Hatton, who told them more about the history of the house and its occupants.

The following morning, Aunt Lucy asked Mr. Hatton to show them the room where the children's toys had been kept in the cupboard. They were mostly made of wood, each one carefully carved, including a Noah's Ark with numerous pairs of animals finished in many colours, a miniature painted rocking horse, and a large dolls' house fully furnished throughout that contained some rather worn rag dolls. Aunt Lucy reminisced nostalgically about her own childhood, when she and her younger sister, Julia's mother, had played with very similar toys in their own nursery.

Julia's eyes met those of Mr. Hatton above her aunt's head, and they exchanged a smile. Indeed, it was with some difficulty that the young people persuaded her aunt to move on to the rest of the house.

"I suggest, Mrs. Harrison, that you might like to inspect the items in the rooms with your niece at more leisure, and see if there is anything that would take your fancy."

For the next two hours, Julia followed her aunt around the ground-floor rooms, and then around the bedrooms above where there were also many items of interest. At her aunt's request, she made a list as they went, enumerating those objects that caught her fancy. After a while, Mr. Hatton sensibly left them to their search, as the notes on Julia's paper grew longer and more detailed. Eventually, they returned to the ground floor, and her aunt sat on the drawing room settee beside Julia, and they went through the list again.

"I have decided," said Aunt Lucy at last, "I would like to have one of the children's toys from the nursery, the carved miniature rocking horse with the dark blue saddle!"

As her aunt had lingered for a long time looking at the toy cupboard, this did not come as a great surprise to Julia, though she did not say so.

At that moment, Mrs. Jones entered, followed by Mr. Hatton,

with the offer of tea or coffee to enable her aunt to recover from her exertions.

"Do not let me be so selfish as to detain you whilst I have my tea, Mr. Hatton, for you said that you would like to take Julia around the house to discuss your ideas for redecorations. Perhaps this is a good moment?"

He agreed. "If you do not object, Mrs. Harrison, as Miss Maitland may have some suggestions for suitable colours that I might consider."

Mr. Hatton took Julia down a step between the old and newer parts of the building into the dining room, which Julia thought was rather dark and oppressive. It seemed to be north-facing, and all the furniture was a very sombre brown.

"I thought perhaps a pale green on the walls in this room, Miss Maitland. It needs a lighter colour, don't you think?"

"I agree. But perhaps picking out the cornice and picture rail with a certain amount of gold?"

He looked doubtful, until she led him over to one of the picture frames that was in just that combination of colours, and contrasted it with another where only the green had been used. Then he acknowledged that she was right.

"We do have a library here in the house, Miss Maitland. Would you like to see that?"

"Of course, for I must not allow my bookish reputation to lapse, sir, you must agree!"

He laughed, remembering their conversation at Norton Place, and led the way through the house to a long room beside the front door.

It was again rather dark and gloomy, with wood panelling on the walls, but especially because the thick curtains were drawn across the windows. A large quantity of dust billowed out into the room as Mr. Hatton pulled one back from the glass, causing him to cough and Julia to draw back in mock alarm.

"I do apologise, Miss Maitland—this room has not been the first priority for Mrs. Jones. I will ask her to attend to it soon. Now, there is something in this room that you may recognise. Please look around you."

He can't mean a book, thought Julia, for there were so many on the shelves on every side, and the titles were difficult to read in the half light, so it must be elsewhere.

He waited as she turned around, scanning the walls, and then back, up and down, until at last she cried out in recognition.

"*La Passerelle*!" she exclaimed, looking up at a framed draw-ing hanging close to the door. It showed what seemed to be a stone wall on each side, with an arch between them bridging the gap, and two figures apparently walking over the divide.

"During your stay here, I will show you where that is situated in the park," he said.

At that moment, they were interrupted by a crash, followed by a dreadful cry of pain, and the sound of running feet. They both turned in alarm and made their way quickly in the direc-tion of the sound. They were met by Mrs. Jones rushing towards them.

"Sir! Miss! Mrs. Harrison has fallen down the step into the dining-room, and her ankle—she is in great pain!"

They found Aunt Lucy lying on the floor below the step, clutching her ankle, which was twisted away from her leg.

Mr. Hatton was immediately decisive. "Mrs. Jones, please tell one of the grooms to ride to Beaminster immediately, to fetch Dr. Bulman, and bring him here directly."

She ran to the front door as Mr. Hatton called to the footman to help him move Aunt Lucy to a chair in the drawing room, whilst Julia found a housemaid and asked her for a cold compress to apply to the ankle until the doctor came. Her aunt was looking very pale, and Julia was not happy with the way the ankle, now resting on a stool, was swelling up to much larger than its normal size even as she watched. She asked the housemaid for a glass of brandy for her aunt, which Mrs. Jones brought with a message that the groom had left for Beaminster as instructed.

Aunt Lucy tried to refuse the brandy, but Mr. Hatton and Julia insisted, and she lay back on the cushions as Julia held her hand to comfort her. Within the hour, the groom returned, closely followed by Dr. Bulman.

Mr. Hatton and Julia withdrew, and waited outside whilst the doctor examined his patient. After about ten minutes, he came out to speak to them in the hall.

"I understand that you are Mrs. Harrison's niece, Miss Maitland? Fortunately, the ankle is not broken, but it is badly twisted and sprained, so your aunt must rest and not walk on it for at least a week." Turning, he said, "I hope that Mrs. Harrison's remaining here for that length of time is no problem, Mr. Hatton?"

"Of course not, she is welcome for as long as it takes for her to recover."

"Then I will return in a few days' time to see how she does. But Mrs. Harrison should not plan to go home until at least next week." And doffing his hat to Julia, and shaking Mr. Hatton's hand, he went out through the front door and rode away.

They found Aunt Lucy in the drawing room, with her ankle tightly bandaged, and sufficiently better to be deeply apologetic about the trouble that she was causing to her host.

He brushed her protestations aside, assuring her that his servants would be only too pleased to be kept busy looking after

Mrs. Harrison. He added that he would be happy to keep Miss Maitland company until Mrs. Harrison was sufficiently recovered to join them.

Her aunt agreed readily to this suggestion and was soon settled in the drawing room with refreshments and books to hand, Mrs. Jones and Martha sitting near her, and a bell at her elbow ready to summon help whenever she needed attention.

"Now, Miss Maitland," said Mr. Hatton, "we have the opportunity to do whatever you wish during the next few days. Do you have any preferences?"

"That is a very wide invitation, sir," she said, smiling. "As the weather is looking rather grey now, perhaps we should stay indoors this afternoon, and that would also enable me to keep an eye on my aunt to make sure that she is not trying to walk anywhere for the moment."

"But of course, that is a very practical suggestion and I agree that we should not go too far for the next day or two."

"Then may I see your ballroom now, Mr. Hatton?" she said, remembering their conversation in the Assembly Rooms at Bath.

"Of course. Please come this way." And he led Julia across the house to a pair of handsome panelled doors set in a recess at the side of the entrance hall. As he pushed them, the hinges creaked and it took all his strength to open the doors.

"I can see that there is a job to be done on these," he said ruefully, as he held one of the doors aside for her to enter the room.

She looked around her and, as he had said, the ballroom was not large; perhaps big enough for about forty people including about half that number dancing in the centre. As with the library, the tall windows were covered by faded drapes keeping out the light and giving the room a rather depressing air.

As though reading her mind, Mr. Hatton said, "This room needs quite a lot done to it, don't you think? But it could be quite delightful with lighter colours on the walls and new curtains on the windows."

Julia agreed. They went across together and pulled some of the drapes away from the windows. Despite the greyish light outside, the ballroom immediately took on a more pleasant aspect.

"Perhaps, when we know each other better, Miss Maitland, you may allow me, with your aunt's permission, to teach you how to dance the waltz?"

Julia hesitated for some few seconds before replying. "It is not, sir, that I do not wish to dance with you, but that particular dance—I believe that I would prefer us to be better acquainted before you show me how we should do the steps together."

There was a long silence before he spoke again, and she expected him to disagree with her, but he did not.

"Let us make a pact then, Miss Maitland. When I know you better, and when I have your aunt's permission to call you by your Christian name, then shall we dance the waltz?"

It was with such relief that Julia considered his answer. It was so pleasant, first, to contemplate having the time to get to know Mr. Hatton better than she did now and, second, that they might be on intimate enough terms that he could use her own name.

"Mr. Hatton, the only thing that really worries me at this moment is that something is going to prevent either of us doing as we wish in the future. But I suppose that I should stand back from that idea, and enjoy the opportunities during the next few days."

"Thank you for that. Now, perhaps we should go and see how your aunt is faring with Mrs. Jones to look after her."

As they walked back across the house, Julia asked him, "Are you enjoying being the owner of a large house, Mr. Hatton?"

"I'm not sure yet, Miss Maitland. I had absolutely no idea, you see, until after Mrs. Hatton's death that I was to inherit the house and the land attached to it. Indeed, my godmother's attorney told me that, until two years ago, the estate was to go to her nephew by marriage. He was the son of her husband Henry's younger brother, but he died young, and he was the last in that family line."

"I have often thought," Julia observed," that inheritance depends so very much on chance, and so very little on merit." Then noting his expression and suddenly remembering Jack Douglas, she added with some embarrassment, "I had in mind the heirs to great families who take it for granted that they should inherit whether they are suitable or not."

"And not either of the sons of a self-made businessman, Miss Maitland?"

Had she not seen the humour in his face, she might have taken him more seriously.

"I am sure that merit can be earned, Mr. Hatton. Do you have some plans for that, now that I can tell that you are becoming so very grand?" Julia could see her aunt watching them from her chaise longue as they entered the room, wondering perhaps what was the source of the amusement that they were sharing.

"Aunt Lucy, would you like to play a game of cards with us? You are going to get very bored just sitting there without some occupation from time to time."

This suggestion commended itself to her aunt and, by various means, the two young people entertained Aunt Lucy for the rest of the day until it was time to go to bed.

On the following morning, Mr. Hatton made some suggestions

after breakfast as to how he and Julia could occupy their time during the next few days.

"Mrs. Harrison, I have various ideas as to what we could do. My godmother established a small school some years ago near the village church, and I'm sure that the teacher would welcome a visit from both of us there. Then I would like to take the opportunity to drive Miss Maitland in my curricle around the grounds and, if you will permit, to give her the opportunity to take the reins."

He looked at Julia and, encouraged by her smile, continued.

"If the weather becomes better, we could walk up the hill that you can see out of the window to the crest, where there is a view of the sea. At some point, I need to have a discussion with my factor, Mr. Whitaker, about the management of the farm; I believe that Miss Maitland has some knowledge of the methods being used at Holkham in Norfolk, which may be of interest to him. And my last idea is that there are a few shops in Beaminster, or perhaps Bridport, that Miss Maitland might like to see and, if you have any personal needs, she could make some purchases for you."

Aunt Lucy said, "That sounds a very entertaining programme, my dear Julia. I am only sorry that I cannot join you, but I have no intention of confining you to the house just because of my stupid accident."

So thus it was that Julia found herself in the company of Mr. Hatton without any interruption for the next few days.

SEVEN

If you are willing, Miss Maitland, I suggest that we go this morning to the village school that I mentioned to you. My godmother appointed Mrs. Whitaker, the wife of the factor whom she hired to run the farm, to be the teacher."

"I should be delighted," said Julia, and she went to get her pelisse and gloves, as the weather was still rather grey.

Mr. Hatton handed Julia up into the curricle, and then went around to the other side to take his place beside her.

Before they started off, Julia said, "This curricle looks to be in very good condition, Mr. Hatton."

He looked at her without expression, then took the reins for the two horses in his hands before he said, "It has been my only purchase so far since I inherited the estate. My father acquired a curricle for my mother when he bought Norton Place, and she taught me to drive it. You may know that not everyone approves of ladies having to handle two horses in a light carriage, as they think it might be too dangerous, but my father did not agree with that view."

"So you purchased a curricle as soon as you knew that Morancourt was to be yours?"

He turned his head and looked at her directly for a moment before saying, "No, Miss Maitland, I purchased the curricle from a coach builder in Bath once I knew that you would be coming to Morancourt. It was here waiting for me when I returned from the city last week."

He hesitated, and then continued, "I wanted to be able to take you out and, if you had not been taught to drive a curricle, hoped that I might be allowed to show you, if you wished that."

For a few moments, Julia found it very difficult to think of a reply to this.

Finally, trying to speak lightly, she said, "That is one of the nicest surprises that anybody could give me. My father did once let me take the reins of a curricle owned by a friend, but only for a few minutes, and for a very short distance. We do not have one ourselves at Banford Hall."

"Then my purchase is already worthwhile. Shall we start now?"

And he called to the footman to take his place on the footplate at the rear of the curricle.

Then Mr. Hatton tightened his grip on the reins and they set off along the drive away from the house. The village was about a mile further along the lane down a narrow valley, and Julia admired the way in which he controlled the horses around the sharp bends and down the slope into the village. Once or twice, he glanced at her, perhaps concerned that he might be driving too fast, but Julia found the journey exhilarating and was sorry when they reached the school gate and she had to get out.

The building was a low thatched structure situated next to the church. It had the appearance of a barn, but with a good number of mullioned windows looking out over the street. They walked up the path to the old timber door and, after Mr. Hatton knocked, he gestured her to go first and Julia entered, to find herself in a simple space with a row of desks at one end and the teacher's table in the centre.

Mrs. Whitaker was sitting at the table, but immediately rose and curtsied to Mr. Hatton. She was a youngish woman, neatly dressed in a blue-grey cotton gown covered by an apron. The children sat wide-eyed in front of her at their desks, looking at the new arrivals. They were between about five and ten years of age, some rather raggedly attired, the boys each with a kerchief knotted around their necks, and the girls wearing aprons.

Mr. Hatton introduced Julia to Mrs. Whitaker, and the teacher gave up her seat to her and invited several of the children to come and sit around them.

"Would it be helpful," said Julia, "if I told them a short story?"

"Please do, Miss Maitland," said Mrs. Whitaker, and she stood with Mr. Hatton by her side whilst Julia explained the tale of Little Red Riding Hood. The children were particularly delighted at the animal noises that Julia made at appropriate points in the story, and she could see Mr. Hatton's considerable amusement at this.

"Now, Mr. Hatton," said Julia, "it's your turn." And he did not need much persuading to tell the children the fable of Cinderella.

After this, some of the girls showed Julia their efforts at needlework, and the boys some models that they had been making. After a few more words with Mrs. Whitaker, the visitors left.

"Did you notice something, Mr. Hatton?" she said as he handed her back into the curricle.

"What was that?" he said, surprised at her tone of voice.

"The boys' kerchiefs, some of them were made of silk. I would not have expected that in a country area, and when their other clothes were mostly very worn and old."

"Are you quite sure, Miss Maitland?"

"Yes, quite sure," she said.

"Perhaps," he said slowly, "Mrs. Whitaker had cut up some old material for them?"

"Perhaps, but the patterns were not all the same, and the silk material looked new to me."

Mr. Hatton looked thoughtful as they drove back along the country lane to Morancourt, where they found Aunt Lucy quite content, doing some needlework and with her injured ankle resting on the chaise longue.

"Ah, there you are, Julia," said her aunt. "A letter came for me whilst you were out. It is from your mother."

"Oh—is there any news of Papa?"

"Not very much new. He is still resting a good part of the day and, you will be pleased to hear, reading some of the books that you chose for him before you left home."

"Does Mama say anything about my travelling with you to Morancourt?"

"Well, yes, she does. She just suggests that you would have had better opportunities to meet more young people in Bath."

Julia made a face, turning her head away as she did so, hoping that Mr. Hatton had not heard or could see her expression. That was a typical comment by her mother, when she was so enjoying herself away from the frivolities and often artificial atmosphere in Bath.

After luncheon, they left Aunt Lucy lying on the chaise longue, collected their outdoor wear, and went out onto the front forecourt of the house.

"I suggest, Miss Maitland, that you take a short turn in the curricle with me now, and try taking the reins. When you are learning, it is always best that the horses are not too fresh. They should be quite calm after our outing this morning to the village school."

She readily agreed, but was surprised that they did not immediately set off.

"There is one thing that you must always remember about a curricle, Miss Maitland. They may be fast-moving, but they are inherently unstable. So there must always be a servant—a footman or someone else—on the footplate at the back to balance the vehicle. Because of the rush of the wind, he cannot hear our conversation. But without him, we would be at risk of overturning, however carefully we drive."

And Mr. Hatton waited whilst the footman took his place before they started off. Then followed one of the most enjoyable hours of Julia's life to date.

Mr. Hatton showed her how to take the reins in her hands and to apply pressure gently to guide the horses first one way and then another, then to bring them smoothly to a halt when she wanted to. To begin with, Julia found this quite difficult, but with practice she found that the horses began to follow her will, and the direction and speed that she wanted.

They took a circuit of the drive from the house past the stables to the gatehouse, and then back to the manor, and then repeated that several times. Finally, Mr. Hatton took the reins again himself and steered the curricle back towards the house. Julia was profuse in her thanks, and was about to get down from the carriage when he asked her to wait for a moment.

After he had dismissed the footman, he said, "Could I ask you, Miss Maitland, whether your mother is much like her sister, your aunt Mrs. Harrison?"

She looked at him for a few moments. "No, not very much.

Of course, it is much easier to be good-humoured and generous with your time when you have plenty of money and no children to worry about, as is the case with my aunt. She is older than my mother, and they are two very different people. I am told that I am much more like my father than Mama. Harriet, my youngest sister, is good fun, and you might find her the most like my aunt of the three of us. It is Sophie, my middle sister, who is more like my mother."

He looked at her without replying for some moments, so she added, "Why do you ask?"

"Only that I have noticed that you seemed more at ease in Bath, and happily here also, than you did in Derbyshire."

"There are many reasons for that, sir," she said. "It has been so much easier to relax here in the West Country, whereas there have been so many more pressures on me lately back at home."

He nodded, then helped her down from the curricle, and they entered the house.

Later that evening, Julia helped her aunt to compose a reply to Mama's letter, which said enough, but not too much, about what they might be currently doing. By mutual consent, her aunt did not mention the accident to her ankle—only that Julia was enjoying meeting all kinds of people in the locality. This might, she thought, be some exaggeration, but it should divert Mama from any ideas of calling her back home when she would much rather stay where she was.

"You once mentioned Holkham in Norfolk, Mr. Coke's house and estate," said Mr. Hatton the following morning. "Have you been there yourself, Miss Maitland?"

"No, I have read about it, but it was my father's factor who went there, at my brother David's suggestion. He came back with so many ideas for improvements to my family's property. As it turned out, with the failure of the bank in Derby, the opportunity to make quite simple changes to the way our land is being used has meant that the income is already increasing from my father's estate. That has been most useful at a time when the money coming from other sources has been reduced." Then she saw his expression. "You are surprised that I know about such things?"

"No—only that any young lady should be interested," he said, rather shamefaced. "I cannot imagine that my mother would have been the same."

"Was she a practical person, Mr. Hatton?"

"In housekeeping, and in house decoration, yes, but she did not have a great curiosity about money or anything new. Rather like Jack—I am sure that you have not forgotten that from your visit to Norton Place!"

"Would I have liked her?"

He thought for a few moments. "In some ways, yes—she loved books, but she was also rather reclusive and shy. That led some people to say that she had a cold manner. Everyone was very surprised, I've been told, when she decided that she wanted to marry my father, for she had far grander suitors. But she recognised in my father a kindness and a generosity of manner lacking in most of the others."

"I liked your father very much," said Julia, "but he said very little to me about your mother, although of course he does not know me very well."

"He was absolutely devastated when she died," said Mr. Hatton. "As you know, I came back from Spain after she passed away, and I have never seen him so distraught. He really did not know what to do with himself. To be fair to Jack, my brother, he had done his best to console him, and it was a comfort to both of them when I returned home."

"Did your father have any problems persuading your mother's relations to allow her to marry him?"

"Her family was not keen on the idea at all. The match did not meet their expectations for the daughter of a baronet, but my father's wealth, and her total determination, finally wore them down. You would approve of that, I would guess?"

Julia gave a wide smile. "But of course, Mr. Hatton!"

She wondered why he paused before replying, but that smile always distracted him, and made his heart skip a beat.

"I hope that you will be impressed," he said, "if I tell you that I have written to Mr. Coke in Norfolk to ask if I may attend the next sheep-shearing and the annual gathering at Holkham, and I plan to take Mr. Whitaker with me. But that will not be for a few months. So will you come with me now to meet him, and explain a little of what he might learn there?"

She readily agreed, and they walked together down the drive and then along a side turning towards the group of farm buildings. There, inside the cattle shed, they found the factor busy with two farmhands to help him, forking over the hay and penning the animals at one end of the shed whilst they did so.

After the introductions, Mr. Hatton said to Mr. Whitaker, "Miss Maitland has some knowledge of the practices used by Mr. Coke at Holkham Hall, John. They are already being employed on her father's land at Banford Hall in Derbyshire."

Julia then explained how her father had changed the type of cattle that he kept on the estate, and that he used oil cake and roots to feed them.

"He has also introduced wheat as a crop where the land is suitable, drilling the ground rather than scattering the seed by hand. That seems to give a much higher yield than the rye grown previously, and he makes much greater use of manure and bones as fertilisers. I have been told that these methods of managing the estate have greatly increased the yields."

"Rather a lot to remember, John," said Mr. Hatton, "but I am told that seeing the practices in action in Norfolk is the best way of understanding it all."

Mr. Whitaker looked very interested, and told Julia that he would be glad to learn more. He then showed her around the farm buildings and explained the areas where repairs and improvements were being considered.

"Where do you and your family live, Mr. Whitaker? We met your wife at the school yesterday, teaching the children," said Julia.

"Our house is further south from here, Miss Maitland, closer to the village and not far from the road towards the sea."

"How old is it, Mr. Whitaker? Is it the same age as Morancourt?"

Mr. Hatton suddenly looked apologetic. "Mr. Whitaker, I should have asked you before whether your house needs any attention?"

"It's an old place, sir. We like it as it is," he replied.

I wonder if his wife agrees that the house does not need attention, thought Julia. If Morancourt needs renovating, surely the servants' homes do as well?

"Would you object," said Julia, "if we call in to see your wife one day?"

"No, of course not, Miss Maitland, if you would like to do that. The school is open only in the mornings, so that the children can help their parents on the land in the later part of the day. So my wife gets home at about one o'clock."

On the way back, Julia asked her host about his opinion of Mr. Whitaker.

"I am not sure. It may be difficult for him to have someone taking a more active interest at such short notice."

"You have told me before that some people don't like change. Perhaps his attitude will improve?"

"Don't mistake me—he is not being rude or surly in his manner. There is just something that I cannot put my finger on for the moment."

Julia considered this. "I would like to go with you and visit their house soon, if you agree?"

He indicated his assent to this idea, and they walked back to the house to find how Aunt Lucy was progressing. Much to their amusement, they found that Mrs. Jones had brought her recipe book from the kitchen and was writing down several ideas suggested by Aunt Lucy for the menus later that week.

"Now, Mrs. Jones, have you a recipe for syllabub? My cook in Bath has the most excellent means of making that."

Mrs. Jones looked suitably impressed, and sent Martha to find more pages to insert in her book to write on.

"Have you told Mrs. Jones about the recipe for Derbyshire pudding, Aunt Lucy?" asked Julia innocently.

Aunt Lucy looked puzzled, and then realised that her niece was hoaxing her. "Julia, you wicked minx! Mr. Hatton, what she means is that she and her sisters love any dessert that is sweet, and especially anything containing lemons."

"Lemons?" he said. "I had some desserts in Spain, when we had time to dine in the towns, that were very enjoyable. But I am afraid that I did not ask the ingredients, though I could guess if you wish."

Thus ensued an entertaining half hour during which Mr. Hatton described the desserts that he remembered, their appearance and taste, and Mrs. Jones and Aunt Lucy made notes, with the intention of experimenting with the recipes once Julia's aunt was more recovered.

"Can we get lemons in Dorset?" said Julia innocently, "I thought perhaps that in these wild country parts—"

Mr. Hatton laughed out loud, for he knew that she was teasing him.

"For that, Miss Maitland, I should drag you to either Beaminster or Bridport, and show you how well provisioned are many of the shops in the towns in this locality. There are several very wealthy farmers, as well as some great estates, within a short drive of here, you know. You will find that the local grocers and provisions shop, Messrs. Pines in Beaminster, has a range of goods to rival that in the London premises of Messrs. Fortnum and Mason in Piccadilly."

"Yes, sir," said Julia very demurely.

There was a message waiting for Mr. Hatton when they got back to the house. He had mentioned previously to Aunt Lucy that an old school friend of his lived nearby and owned a large estate. The suggestion was that Mr. Hatton should go with his friend to an assembly and dance at the Rooms in Beaminster in a few days time, and that Julia would be welcome to accompany him if she wished.

"Mrs. Harrison, my friend James Lindsay tells me in this letter that he will have a party of about twelve young people going to Beaminster on Saturday night. May I reply that we will go? His mother will be attending to chaperone the young ladies, so I am sure that she would look after Miss Maitland as well, if that is acceptable to you?"

"As you have known the family for a long time, Mr. Hatton, of course I will agree."

"I could send the reply by my groom, but alternatively I could take Miss Maitland with me in the carriage tomorrow morning to deliver the letter in person, so that she has the opportunity to meet some of the family before Saturday evening. May we do that?"

After looking at Julia to be sure that she liked the idea, Aunt Lucy readily agreed.

Dinner that evening included some dishes made from recipes that had been given to Mrs. Jones by Aunt Lucy, and they were pronounced a great success. After the rather elaborate meals that they had had on some occasions in Bath, Julia found the new recipes a refreshing change. Mrs. Jones was delighted at the praise that she received and promised Mr. Hatton that she and the cook would redouble their efforts to widen their culinary repertoire.

"How is your ankle now, Aunt Lucy? Is it feeling better at all?" said Julia. She had noticed that her aunt had ventured once or twice to take a few short steps around the chaise longue, to ease her stiffness after sitting for so long.

"I believe that it is a little more comfortable, thank you, my dear," said her aunt, "but I will not venture very far without Mrs. Jones or Martha beside me until the doctor returns, for I do not wish to compromise my recovery. I do promise you that I will not risk anything tomorrow morning, whilst you are visiting Mr. Lindsay at his house."

"I beg your pardon, Mrs. Harrison," said Mr. Hatton, "I should have made it clear that it is Sir James Lindsay, for his late father was a baronet."

Her aunt's pleasure at hearing of this title reminded Julia forcibly of her mother, except for the difference that her aunt did not press the importance of the title upon her niece. But Julia noticed Mr. Hatton observing her reaction with a rather amused expression and diagnosed (correctly) that he was thinking of her description of her Mama.

After they had left Aunt Lucy to Martha's ministrations before bed, Mr. Hatton escorted her to the foot of the stairs and said, "Miss Maitland, I do apologise. I should not have made that comparison between your aunt and your mother, even though I said nothing explicit to you."

"Mr. Hatton, I am getting quite worried."

He immediately looked rather concerned but, before he could say more, Julia continued, "that we are getting to be too good at reading each other's minds!"

He visibly relaxed and acknowledged her joke with a smile. He then took himself in hand and bowed formally to her before she turned to go up the stairs to bed.

The following morning, Mr. Hatton told Aunt Lucy, "We will take the carriage, Mrs. Harrison, as some of the lanes on the way to my friend's house are rather uneven and not suitable for the curricle. We should be back with you by mid-afternoon at the latest."

The weather had become a little more overcast, but Mr. Hatton asked the coachman to put the hood of the carriage down so that Julia could see better.

"I have asked him to take us on the road via Bridport, so that you may see the Rope Walks there."

"What are Rope Walks?" asked Julia, "I have never heard the term."

"You will see when we reach Bridport. Ropes have been made in this part of Dorset for many hundreds of years, mainly for the Navy. In times of war, the trade has been very important in the history of the nation. The crops that are needed for making rope, flax, and hemp, are grown in the fields all over this area of South Dorset. If you look to both sides of the road, you will see them."

Julia gave the fields more detailed attention after this remark, and saw some of the flax growing strongly on the slopes of the valley.

"Flax and hemp can be very significant in the income of an estate," Mr. Hatton said as they neared Bridport. "My friend Sir James, and his family before him, have been active in the trade, especially since the Bounties Act provided subsidies for growing the crops. That was because of the interruptions to the other supplies from America and the Continent by the war."

"Are those crops grown at Morancourt?"

"Not at present, as far as I am aware. My friend will be able to advise me. I don't yet know whether any of the land is suitable."

When they arrived in Bridport, they left the carriage on a side road, and Mr. Hatton took Julia to see the rope walks in some of the lanes leading off the wide streets, where the rope makers were hard at work. Long lengths of flax, already twisted into strands, were being combined with others, all tied to posts before the workers twisted them at one end to form the long thick ropes, wider than a man's wrist.

"King John commanded the townspeople about five hundred years ago, at the time of another war with France, to 'make ropes by night and day.' Many nets are made around here as well, for the fishermen and the Navy ships. So you will understand that much of the prosperity of the town is founded on those trades—that, and some smuggling, according to my friend James. And no, I did not read any of that in the *Bridport News*, which as you may guess is the local newspaper, Miss Maitland!"

Julia laughed, remembering their conversation on the canal

boat. "Perhaps your godmother, Mrs. Hatton, might have told you when you were young?"

"Indeed." And he smiled at her in the way that so touched her heart.

"It certainly looks to be a prosperous town," said Julia, admiring the fine buildings on each side of the main street as they returned to the carriage and took their seats, and Mr. Hatton told the coachman to continue their journey.

When they reached the Lindsays' estate, they could see the large stone house set on the slope of the hill ahead, built in the style fashionable in the late 1780s, and set back behind a large lake. When the carriage reached the portico, Mr. Hatton handed Julia out onto the gravel and invited her to look at the view before they entered the house. There was a most attractive panorama over the green parkland and the lake and beyond across the Marshwood Vale. In the distance they could see the deep blue of the sea on the coast.

The handsome oak doors to the house were opened by a smartly dressed footman, who seemed to be expecting them. As the butler led them through the hall, they could hear voices in the drawing room beyond.

"Kit, how good it is to see you again! And this must be Miss Maitland? You are very welcome."

Without doubt, this must be James Lindsay, thought Julia. He was a pleasant young man with a shock of red hair, and about the same height as Mr. Hatton, dressed in a subdued style appropriate for a country location. Sitting beyond him were two older ladies, and their host turned to them to make the introductions.

"Kit, you know my mother, of course. Miss Maitland, this is my mother, Lady Lindsay, and her sister, Mrs. Jepson."

Lady Lindsay was a fine-looking woman in an elegant gown

and with her neatly dressed greying hair still tinged with the red that her son had inherited. Mrs. Jepson, by contrast, had faded brown curls, which were arranged in a rather untidy style, and to Julia's eyes she was wearing a rather fussy and old-fashioned dress.

"Kit, congratulations on your new inheritance! I was so delighted to hear the news from James. I know of the estate, although I have never been there."

"Thank you, ma'am. It is all very new to me at present, but I look forward to welcoming you to Morancourt. I am hoping that James can advise me on various matters relating to the use of the land, once I have had time to discover what needs to be done."

Lady Lindsay turned to Julia.

"I should be delighted to be your chaperone in Beaminster on Saturday evening, Miss Maitland. I dare say that you will not need much protection amongst the pleasant group of young people who will be attending the occasion, but I shall be very pleased to be of assistance. My sister is staying with me for a few days, before returning to her home near Yeovil, and so will be accompanying us."

Mrs. Jepson said very little, but seemed to be a pleasant woman, although of no great intellect. After a few more minutes of conversation, Lady Lindsay suggested that her son might show Miss Maitland parts of the house, and so Julia went with Mr. Hatton and his friend back into the hall.

"I understand, Sir James, that you went to school with Mr. Hatton. I would dearly love to know what kind of a schoolboy he was!"

"Very determined, Miss Maitland, and very good at his books, too, unlike me."

"You are too hard on yourself, my friend," said Mr. Hatton, "for you gained a place at Oxford at the same time as I did."

Julia looked surprised, but, before she could put the question, Mr. Hatton answered her. "I decided not to go to Oxford, Miss Maitland, much to my mother's regret, but to take up a commission in the regiment instead. I saw little future for myself as a clergyman, and the benefit of a degree in any other profession that I might pursue seemed very limited."

"Does your aunt have any children, Sir James? Jepson is an unusual name, and I met a young man of that surname in Bath a little while ago."

"Yes, Miss Maitland, I have three cousins. Patrick is the youngest; his two elder sisters are both married and living some distance away now."

On the way back to Morancourt, Mr. Hatton said, "Why did you ask whether my aunt had any children?"

Julia thought quickly. "As I said, Jepson seems rather an unusual name."

Mr. Hatton gave her a long look, and Julia realised that he was well aware that she had not told him the whole story, but he didn't question her anymore.

EIGHT

The rest of that day was rather wet, and Julia spent most of the evening with her aunt. They jointly composed a letter to Emily Brandon, for she was due to return to Cressborough Castle within the next few days. From that activity, her aunt moved on to ask about more details of the Brandon family, but fortunately Mr. Hatton had left them by that time to attend to some business in his study, so that Julia did not have to take too much care in what she said.

The next day was Friday, and Mr. Hatton proposed that he and Julia should take the carriage to Eggardon Hill, an earthwork some distance to the east of Morancourt that was thought to be very old, and from which he said fine views could be obtained.

The journey did not take too long. Mr. Hatton explained that the farm there below Eggardon Hill was reputed to have been bought at the end of the previous century by one of the most successful smugglers in Dorset, Isaac Gulliver. A group of trees was said to have been planted on the hilltop to act as a beacon for ships coming along the Channel to bring contraband goods ashore.

"That was what Mr. Henry Hatton told me when I was young, but I don't know whether it's true. The Gulliver family may still own the farm, and I thought that it might be useful to have a look, although we can pretend that we have just come to observe the scenery."

This, thought Julia, is much more interesting than sitting at home in Derbyshire doing needlework, or reading a book in my father's library.

As though being aware of her thoughts, Mr. Hatton said, "It might be very dangerous if we encounter the wrong people, so please do be careful what you say if we should meet anyone."

However, when they had left the carriage at the end of the track and walked up to the highest point, at first they found only the stumps of a group of trees, and visible in the distance at a lower level, there was an old farmhouse, which seemed to be defended by a group of barking dogs. Mr. Hatton did not venture in that direction, but pointed out to Julia various landmarks that could be seen from the vantage point, including a wide panorama of the coastline.

It was as they turned to walk back to the carriage that they found a broad-shouldered man of middle height and with sparse grey hair standing on the path some distance ahead, looking directly at them. As they came closer, Julia could see that his coat was of good quality, buttoned high against the wind, and his hands were well kept, as though he was not used to manual labour.

"Good day to you, sir," he said in a local accent, entering into conversation with Mr. Hatton and introducing himself as the priest from the village church in Burton Bradstock. He acknowledged some acquaintance with the Lindsay family, and after some time Mr. Hatton turned the discussion adroitly towards the subject of smuggling.

"Don't you believe everything that you have heard about Isaac Gulliver, sir. He is in late middle age now, but was never a dangerous or violent man, just very skilful at his trade. It is some of those others in a new group operating closer to Bridport who are causing more trouble now."

Julia took more interest in the conversation at this point, since Mr. Hatton's expression remained calm and apparently disinterested.

"Why is that?" she asked.

"They seem to be in a hurry to make a lot of money very quickly, Miss, and I've heard that anyone getting in their way can find that they get a very sore head for their pains!"

"Oh! I see."

"And they are going for the very valuable fancy stuff, wines and silks—not tobacco or any of the other goods that sell so well around here." The stranger suddenly recollected himself and changed the subject, inquiring where Mr. Hatton and his lady companion had come from. Mr. Hatton made a noncommittal reply, and shortly afterwards, they parted, with the priest making his way on towards the top of the hill.

After Mr. Hatton had handed her back into the carriage, Julia remarked that she had noticed that all the tracks visible from the top of the hill had seemed to be very well used.

"Yes," said Mr. Hatton, "and I wonder who by—our new acquaintance, perhaps?"

"Do you mean that he was not the priest, but a smuggler?"

"Perhaps it doesn't matter, Miss Maitland. But it was interesting what he said about a new group near Bridport. I think I shall make some discreet enquiries of James Lindsay tomorrow."

In their absence, Dr. Bulman had called to see Aunt Lucy, and the news was good. If her ankle continued to improve, she could consider returning home in a few days' time.

Julia had almost forgotten about the social event to which

Lady Lindsay had invited her on Saturday evening, but Aunt Lucy definitely had not. Although she was not as managing as Julia's mother, she did ask her niece all the details of what she was proposing to wear, including which dress, which shoes, and which jewellery.

On the following evening, Martha was summoned to dress Julia's curls in a fashionable style, and all the fussing over her appearance caused her to think that the enjoyment of the evening might be destroyed. However, the pleasure of descending the stairs at Morancourt and finding Mr. Hatton waiting for her in the hall also wearing his best hinted at the delights to come.

Her cheeks were flushed with excitement, and her golden-brown hair was complemented by the colour of her new dress and the handsome necklace that Aunt Lucy had suggested that she should borrow for the evening.

"May I say, Miss Maitland, that you are looking particularly fine this evening?"

"Not 'very overdressed,' as you once remarked about some young ladies in Bath, sir?"

He laughed at the recollection, and said, "No, definitely not, Miss Maitland!"

The journey to Beaminster did not seem to take very long, and there they found Lady Lindsay and the rest of her party waiting for them. They ascended to the upper rooms, where a local band was playing a lively jig for the assembled company. Sir James immediately invited Julia to take the floor with him, and he proved to be a good dancer, with a light step and amusing conversation.

"My cousin Patrick often comes to this kind of assembly when he is at home, but he sent a message to my aunt to say that he had been detained."

"What does your cousin do, Sir James?" Julia said. "Does he manage the family estate, or is he in the army?"

"Neither, Miss Maitland. His father, my uncle by marriage, is still alive and well and in charge of his estate, but he does not often travel to visit us; Mrs. Jepson comes on her own. I'm not sure where my cousin goes. I know that he gets a reasonable allowance from his father, but he was not particularly interested in book learning at school, so did not go to university. I assume that he spends a good part of his time in town."

All that accords, thought Julia, with what I know already about Mr. Jepson. And maybe he is getting short of money for the same reasons as Dominic Brandon is, too much gambling and high living. That reminded her to ask another question.

"Have you heard of the Brandon family, Sir James? I am friendly with their cousin Emily, who lives with them in Derbyshire."

"No, I believe not, but Derbyshire is a long way from here, as you will agree. How is my friend Kit finding his new role as Master of Morancourt? He has seemed very contented since he came into his inheritance last month."

"You know him so much better than I, sir, but it must be a pleasure to find yourself in a situation that you might only have dreamt of previously."

She then asked Sir James whether he was keen on hunting, for she had heard mention of the South Dorset and the Cattistock as being famous packs of foxhounds in South Dorset.

"That's true, Miss Maitland. You are well informed. Both hunts are currently led by Squire Farquharson. I do hunt, when I have time, but I'm not so sure that Kit will do so, since he would be better to avoid injuring his leg again. From what he has told me, it is his brother Jack who prefers hunting."

Julia was about to agree when she remembered that Sir James did not know that she had ever met Jack Douglas, or indeed his father.

"Does anyone in your family hunt in Derbyshire, Miss Maitland?"

"No. My father used to, with my elder brother. But Papa is not well enough now." She could not go on, but found that she did not need to.

"I was very sorry to hear from Kit that your brother was killed at Badajoz," he said gravely.

She thanked him for his sentiments, but by this time the dance was coming to an end, and Mr. Hatton came forward to claim her hand for the next.

He was regarding her with an amused expression and, sure enough, he wanted to know why Julia had been questioning his friend with such persistence. She told him what Sir James had said about his cousin Patrick.

"I didn't think, Miss Maitland, that Mrs. Jepson seemed to be a particularly alert person. Although I had visited the Lindsays several times whilst I was at school with James, I had not met her before. If Patrick Jepson is like her, he may not be very exciting company."

Whilst they had been having this conversation, Julia had noticed that Mr. Hatton had been looking intently across the room at a swarthy gentleman who was standing by the wall in deep conversation with another man.

"Who is that, Mr. Hatton?" said Julia. "Do you know him?"

"No, or at least I don't know what his name is. He was pointed out to me earlier as having some involvement in the local smuggling ring. Apparently, he has a finger in every pie, especially where there is money to be made, and anything to do with obtaining scarce goods in Bridport or in the Marshwood Vale is known to him."

For the rest of the dance, when an opportunity came, Julia tried to look discreetly at this mysterious man who certainly seemed to have little interest in joining in the dance or in circulating to meet any of the other people in the room. There was something familiar about him, despite the fact that she was sure that she had never met him before. What was it? It was only as the music drew to a close that she realised—the man had the same unusually shaped ears as she had noticed on Patrick Jepson.

She ventured to mention this to Mr. Hatton, thinking that he would dismiss it as being fanciful.

But to her surprise he said, "That would explain something that James once told me about his cousin. Apparently Patrick has an older half brother, Frank, who lives near here, the result of a youthful liaison between his father and a local girl. That was before Mr. Jepson met and married my mother's sister. I understand that Patrick meets up with Frank Jepson from time to time. That may be one reason why the father keeps away from the area—not too anxious to be reminded about his follies as a young man, I imagine."

"Oh, really, and you think that's who that gentleman might be?"

"Yes, if you are correct about a family resemblance, although maybe not a 'gentle' man!"

"Do you think that Mrs. Jepson knows anything about him?"

Mr. Hatton said that he thought not, but that Sir James Lindsay might able to obtain more information.

With several pleasant young men in Lady Lindsay's party, Julia found herself dancing every dance, and it was almost midnight before she and Mr. Hatton said good-bye to their new friends and his carriage took them home to Morancourt.

Julia slept late the following morning after all her exertions, and it was well past the time for breakfast before she dressed and descended the stairs. Rather than go into the dining room, she went across the hall and out of the front door. As she did so, Mr. Hatton came into view along the drive with Mr. Whitaker and an older man whom Julia had not seen before. The two other men stopped some distance short of the front door, deep in conversation, but Mr. Hatton continued and greeted her warmly.

"Who is that talking with Mr. Whitaker, Mr. Hatton?"

He looked surprised, then said, "Of course, I had forgotten that you had not met Mr. Jones. I have known him since I first visited my godmother and her husband, Henry, at Morancourt with my mother when I was quite young. As you can see, he is getting on in years now, and so my godmother hired Mr. Whitaker some two years ago to run the farm, and she transferred Mr. Jones to lighter duties, caring only for the park."

"I am a little surprised that Mrs. Jones has never talked about him."

"They have a house in the village, which is owned by the estate. He does not often come up to the manor house nowadays, at least I haven't seen him here recently."

Julia took this opportunity to ask Mr. Hatton another question. "I imagine that your father, Mr. Douglas, must have been delighted at the news of your inheritance?"

Mr. Hatton hesitated, then said, "At this present moment, he knows nothing at all about my inheritance."

Julia looked at him blankly. "He knows nothing about it?"

"I was going to write to Norton Place last month, to invite my father to come down to Dorset. I favoured the notion of breaking the good news to him in person, once he had arrived and could see the estate for himself. But it was at that same time that I wrote to the several legatees named in my godmother's will. As a consequence, I made my visit to Bath, and met Mrs. Harrison, and you."

Julia looked at him intently and waited for him to continue.

"When I thought it through, I realised that there was a serious conflict. In my father's eyes, at least in principle, my brother is a potential suitor for you. Therefore, I could see no way in which my father could be here at the same time as you without all sorts of problems arising."

"I see," said Julia. "I had not thought of that."

"As I say, it has been very difficult. Or perhaps I should say that it could have been difficult. But when I wrote to my father to say that I would not be back in Derbyshire for some weeks, he wrote back in a very gracious way and encouraged me not to worry about it. He said that it would be beneficial—he sounded just like your Aunt Lucy—for me to meet more new people and to have a change of scene."

"So when do you intend to invite your father to visit, Mr. Hatton?"

"I am planning to go to Bath in a week or so, and to meet him there with my carriage."

Julia looked very surprised. "Would he not travel from Derbyshire to Morancourt in his own conveyance?"

"No!" He laughed. "He could, of course, easily afford to do so, but my father is a true Yorkshireman, brought up to be very careful with money, and he considers it much better value to travel with his valet by the stagecoach."

Julia could not help but laugh with him. Then she said, "Tell me, Mr. Hatton, for I do not believe that Papa ever mentioned it, in what business was your father occupied before he retired to Norton Place?"

"I'm not sure that he is retired, in the sense that you mention. He purchased the property there some fifteen years ago, or perhaps it is a longer time than that now. He travels into Leeds and Derby regularly to discuss business with his managers at the mills. They manufacture various types of woollens, and also some cotton fabrics more recently."

"Have you yourself ever had anything to do with that business?"

"No, not really. My mother was particularly keen that my brother and I should never have a direct connection with trade, for she feared that it would adversely affect our prospects in the future."

"I'm surprised that she should be so concerned about that."

"Perhaps it was a rather severe reaction. But it was clear that my father had made his fortune, sufficient to buy Norton Place and to settle money on both of us to give us some means of independent living, so he promised her that neither of us would have anything to do with the business in the future unless some very serious situation arose to make it necessary."

"I suppose that I should understand that," said Julia, "for my family has been settled comfortably for many years at Banford Hall, and I have no experience of any other kind of life."

He looked grave as he answered, "My mother had a similar view to yours, I believe."

"At least she did not want you to marry the daughter of an earl?"

He laughed and said, "Perhaps, if my mother were still here to advise me, she might consider that a very good idea, provided of course that the earl was very wealthy, and the daughter had a large dowry."

I wonder, thought Julia to herself, whether I should really be joking in this way about something that I would detest so much. If Mama were here, she would not find it funny.

That afternoon, Julia was on her way back from selecting a book in the library when she came across Martha in the hall. When she saw Julia, she turned her head away, but not before Julia had seen that she appeared to be crying. Before Martha could open the door to the kitchen, Julia called her back.

"Martha, whatever is the matter?"

Martha reluctantly closed the door and returned to the centre of the hall. But she had to be pressed with the same question twice before she replied, "Will you promise not to tell Mrs. Harrison, Miss?"

"Of course, if that is very important to you. What can it be that is upsetting you so much?"

Eventually Julia persuaded Martha to explain.

"It's my brother Jem, Miss. He's in the kitchen. He's hurt his leg badly, Miss. He says that he dropped a tool on it in the farmyard, Miss. At least, that is what I thought he said." This last statement was made with very little conviction.

When Julia made it clear that she intended to inspect the young man and the wound herself, Martha was clearly very apprehensive. However, when Julia reached the kitchen, Mrs. Jones was there, apparently unconcerned as she tended the leg of a fair-haired young man, roughly dressed in a worn jacket and leggings tied up with string.

She looked up as they arrived and said, quite calmly, "This is Jem, Miss Maitland, one of the farm workers. My husband found him in this state, but I don't think he's done himself any serious harm."

Martha looked at Julia imploringly, and she realised that Mrs. Jones had not been told that Jem was related to Mrs. Harrison's maid.

"Can I be of any use, Mrs. Jones? Martha was upset to see the wound, though I'm sure that you are doing all that can be done."

"No, Miss Maitland, it's very kind of you to take an interest. But I am using a local remedy—sphagnum moss mixed with garlic juice—as a poultice. It is an old country method, but it usually works very well."

Julia made a mental note of this recipe, which she had not heard before.

Jem Fisher looked white-faced, and turned his head away from them as Mrs. Jones applied the poultice to the leg. He did not seem to want to recognise Martha or to make any attempt to speak to either of them.

"Mrs. Jones, you will let me know if you need to send for anything from Beaminster or Bridport?"

"Of course, Miss Maitland, but I should have everything that we need here."

Julia took Martha firmly by the arm and out of the kitchen to a quiet corner in the corridor.

"Did you know that Jem was working in this area, Martha?"

"No, Miss."

"Why did he not acknowledge you as his sister? Do you know what work he's doing?"

"I don't know, Miss."

"Very well," said Julia, thoughtfully. "It might be best if you say nothing about this at present to Mrs. Harrison. I will make inquiries, but only of Mrs. Jones. You should not do anything yourself."

"No, Miss," said Martha, her eyes looking remarkably like those of a frightened rabbit as she darted off upstairs.

Julia debated with herself whether to mention this incident to Aunt Lucy, or to Mr. Hatton, but decided that it would be better to do so when she knew more.

After Aunt Lucy had gone to bed that evening, Julia went back to the kitchen and found Mrs. Jones supervising the maids, who were clearing up the dinner plates and scouring the cooking pans.

"Mrs. Jones, do you know when Mr. Whitaker first employed that young man?"

"No, Miss Maitland. My husband said that he worked on the farm, although I haven't seen him around myself. Most of the farm workers come from the village, or live in one of the estate houses owned by Mrs. Hatton—I mean young Mr. Hatton now, of course."

"And his name is Jem, I think you said?"

"That's what my husband told me when he carried him into the kitchen. He's taken him back to the village now on the cart."

Julia thanked her, and left the matter there.

On the following morning, Julia could not find Mr. Hatton anywhere. Neither Mrs. Jones nor Aunt Lucy could tell her where he was. Julia fetched her walking boots, put on her drab pelisse, and decided to set out along the track towards the farm buildings. She was within a short distance of her destination when she was surprised to see Mr. Jones running towards her.

"Miss Maitland," he said, trying to catch his breath at the same time, "please come with me. It's Mr. Hatton. We had been walking together along the path, and he was ahead of me as it narrowed along a bend. Then I heard shouting and found that the smugglers had pushed him to the ground before they disappeared into the woods!"

He would not explain further, and urgently pressed her to go on with him. Just before they got to the farm buildings, on the last bend in the track, he suddenly swerved into bushes on the left, onto a well-worn path concealed from view on both sides. After about fifty yards, they came upon Mr. Hatton sitting on the ground with his clothes dishevelled and rubbing his head as though badly dazed.

"Here's Miss Maitland, sir," her companion said. "You just walk slowly back with her, Mr. Hatton, and you should be fine."

Mr. Jones helped him to his feet. Then he doffed his cap to Julia and left them, walking quickly in the direction of the sea.

Mr. Hatton looked at Julia ruefully and said, "I told you to be careful, but did not take my own advice!"

"What happened?" said Julia, relieved that he seemed to be speaking sensibly.

"We were walking along the track—Mr. Jones and I—and decided to take this side route, so that we would not be seen. Then three fellows whom I have never seen before came upon me and pushed me aside very roughly, shouting and threatening me. One said in French that I should say nothing about having seen them here. I was interested that neither of the other two seemed to have a local accent."

"Do you speak French fluently?"

"Quite well—my mother had a French governess when she was young, and she in turn taught me. Certainly, I speak French much better than I do Spanish."

"You may have been lucky—the incident could have been much worse!"

"Yes, you are right. I said nothing to them, and I don't think they had any idea who I was. As you may note, I am not dressed as they might have expected a landowner to be."

"No, I see what you mean." Julia laughed, looking at his lack of a coat or neckcloth, and the plain cut of his leggings with a simple white shirt.

"Mr. Jones was walking some distance behind me because there was no width on the path for us both at that point, so they did not catch sight of him before they took another route to get away."

"Do you wish me to support you as far as the house?" Julia asked.

"No, best not," he replied, "though I am obliged to you for your offer. I believe that I am just winded, and shall be fine in a short while."

So they walked slowly back together to the manor house, where Mr. Hatton was able to enter unobtrusively and go up to his room without being observed.

Later that day, Julia went to find Aunt Lucy. "I was thinking of going into Beaminster now with Martha, dear Aunt. Mr. Hatton has offered me the use of his carriage. Do you have any commissions that we can get for you?"

"Well, my dear, Mrs. Jones was mentioning the Blue Vinney cheese to me, which I am told is made locally from skimmed milk and is very palatable. Can you go to the grocers for that whilst you are in the town? And I would fancy some local bread, and perhaps some lemons for those desserts that you were talking about to Mr. Hatton—the ones from Derbyshire."

"Of course, Aunt," said Julia.

On the journey with Martha beside her, and now that she knew what to look for, Julia could see the many fields of flax and hemp alongside the road as they travelled towards the town. Where there were streams in the fields, she could see the dams sometimes made across them to form ponds, which Mr. Hatton had explained were used to soak or "ret" the hemp and flax fibres to soften them. She remembered that he had told her that one of the main products manufactured in Beaminster itself was sailcloth. Like rope, that material was also made from hemp.

The coachman let them down in the corner of the square, saying that they would find Pines, the grocers' shop, along the road on the right in Fleet Street, and he agreed to be back with the carriage to pick them up in about an hour's time.

Pines proved to be a delightful emporium, with a tall bow-fronted window on each side of the stone entrance porch, and the date of 1780 engraved over the main door. Inside, several shop assistants were busy behind the long mahogany counter, serving customers and measuring out flour, sugar, and spices from the jars on the high shelves fixed to the wall behind them. As Mr. Hatton had told her, the range of goods seemed to be as great as in many much grander establishments in Bath and London. Julia chose the various purchases sought by Aunt Lucy, paid for them, and gave them to Martha to carry.

It was after they had returned to the square and were looking in the windows of the other shops that Julia glanced across the street and saw Patrick Jepson alighting from the Bridport coach in front of the White Hart public house. Waiting for him on the paved sideway was the man she had been told might be his half brother, Frank. As she watched, the two walked away together and turned down the road past the Eight Bells Inn leading to St. Mary's Church, and Julia lost sight of them just as Mr. Hatton's carriage arrived for the return journey to Morancourt.

NINE

The next afternoon, Julia went with Mr. Hatton to visit the Whitakers' farmhouse. This time, she had declined his invitation to take the reins of the curricle, on the grounds that she had no familiarity with the route.

The farmhouse was situated much nearer to the sea than the manor itself, and lay low in a fold of the hills, so that the coast was not visible as they alighted and walked towards the front door. The house was built in roughly cut local stone, with the walls partly covered with a green climbing plant. It seemed that Mrs. Whitaker might have been expecting their arrival, for she opened the old oak door almost as soon as they had knocked.

The ceilings inside were low, and Julia guessed that the house was the same age as the older part of the manor house at Morancourt. The sitting room smelt rather damp, and the paintwork and some of the floorboards were worn and in need of attention. The kitchen and scullery were small and dark, so that Julia did not realise for some moments that there were two small children there. The elder, a girl, she recognised from their visit to the school. The younger, a small boy, was playing on the floor with a little puppy.

Mrs. Whitaker answered Julia's unspoken question. "My mother looks after him in the village in the mornings whilst I teach at the school, Miss Maitland. Fortunately he is very good."

After looking around the rooms on the ground floor, Mr. Hatton commented, "Well, Mrs. Whitaker, I am very glad that I came, for it is clear that we need to have some work done here to make your kitchen brighter and easier to use. If you would like to ask Mr. Whitaker to take some measurements, I shall consult Miss Maitland, and we will make some suggestions to discuss with you both."

Mrs. Whitaker was delighted and asked them to look around the upstairs rooms as well, where Mr. Hatton made more notes whilst Julia talked to Mrs. Whitaker.

"I thought that the children in the school were very neatly dressed."

"Thank you, Miss Maitland. Some have only one set of clothes, but most of the boys were given new neckerchiefs recently by a man in the village, which made them feel very smart!"

Julia nodded, and Mr. Hatton paused for a moment whilst writing his notes to listen to this remark. After a few more minutes, they said a cordial farewell to Mrs. Whitaker and left the house.

"Now," he said to Julia, "if we went this way, we would go through the village, but the other way—let's try that." He handed her up into the curricle, and then took his own place and turned the horses along the other track. Soon they could see the sea on their right, and in the distance the roofs of some farm buildings straight ahead of them. Suddenly, Mr. Hatton pulled hard on the reins and brought the curricle to a halt.

"What is it?" said Julia, startled by the abrupt action.

"Look down there, Miss Maitland," said Mr. Hatton very quietly so as not to be overheard by the groom standing on the footplate behind them. He pointed to the east towards the sea, and she saw that there was a well-worn route leading from the track they were following across a field down into a side valley.

"I wonder where that goes?" said Julia quietly in reply. "It looks surprisingly well used."

"Not to the village, so maybe to the seashore. But," he said, looking down at his well-pressed breeches and Julia's neat dress and shoes, "neither of us is dressed for hill-climbing or mountaineering this afternoon. We can look another day, or at least I can," and without further comment he took the curricle on and pulled up the horses at the end of the track, which stopped short of some more farm buildings by about a hundred yards. There again, there were signs of foot traffic from the end of the track towards the old structures.

"Do you think that we have the beginnings of a mystery here?" Julia whispered.

"Perhaps, or it could just be some of the labourers using the buildings as a shelter in wet weather," he replied in an undertone, and he turned the curricle with a sure hand on the reins back onto the route that they had come, and on past the farmhouse again towards Morancourt.

On Wednesday morning, the weather showed a partly blue sky, although a stiff breeze was developing off the sea beyond the crest of the hill. After settling Aunt Lucy in the salon with the help of Martha and Mrs. Jones, Julia fetched her warm white pelisse and her old boots and met Mr. Hatton at the front door, ready to walk with him across the park to the view that he had promised her beyond the hill. He was wearing a long black cloak with several capes over his day attire, as a protection from the wind.

As they made their way together on a rough track alongside a boundary wall leading towards the hill, Mr. Hatton suddenly said, "Do you know Dominic Brandon well? I have heard many things about him—not all of them good. Is your mother very anxious that he should be a serious suitor for you?"

"Perhaps. He is not the only young man she favours. I really prefer not to think about him."

"There are many other young gentlemen in Derbyshire who you might prefer?"

"Do you include your brother in that?" Julia replied.

"Jack? No, I cannot see you marrying him. Chalk and cheese, that would be. But, if that did ever occur, I would not be able to watch you living together."

That is very close to making me a declaration, thought Julia.

"I hope, Mr. Hatton, that you are not trying to organise my life for me?" she replied, trying to speak lightly.

"I'm afraid that I cannot avoid some degree of self-interest in the matter, Miss Maitland."

She had been looking straight ahead during this exchange, but ventured a sideways glance, to find that his green eyes were regarding her with an expression that she could not quite fathom.

"I do wish that I had known you for longer, Miss Maitland, as you do the Brandon family. I sometimes find it very difficult to make out what you might be thinking."

"I have not sought to deceive you, sir. There are few people in the world, I have found, whom I can really rely on and trust—my father is one, and my youngest sister, Harriet, another. And I believe that I have trusted you to tell me the truth from the beginning of our acquaintance. That gives so much ease, does it not?"

He did not reply and, after a short interval of silence, she went on. "Emily Brandon is also someone I can rely on, although

I sometimes find that she is easily diverted when I am trying to get her to take matters seriously."

He laughed out loud. "I agree, for I noticed in Bath that she always said exactly what she thought, whoever was around to hear her. But she is a pretty girl with a pleasant personality, and certainly attracted a great deal of attention from young men wherever she went."

Julia was annoyed with herself to feel a tinge of jealousy at his comment, which was quite irrational, since everything he had just said about Emily was true and confirmed her own perceptions.

Then he added, "But you are unique, Miss Maitland, in my experience. I have never met anyone in my life before whom I have liked and admired so much."

Julia blushed to the roots of her hair and could not think of anything to say.

During this conversation, they had been walking closer and closer to the crest of the hill. On their right there were ridges at intervals across the slope of the ground, creating narrow pathways.

"What are those, Mr. Hatton?"

"Lynchets—they are called strip lynchets. Some people say that they arose over time by ploughing the ground. Others take the view that they were created deliberately many years ago to prevent the farmers and their stock from slipping down the slope and to reduce the erosion of the soil. They are quite common in this part of Dorset."

"Some of the ground above the edge of that lynchet looks as though it has been ploughed recently," observed Julia, "so perhaps they are still in use."

They continued to walk further up the hill for a few more

minutes. Then, just before they got to the top of the slope, Mr. Hatton asked her to stop walking.

"Now, Miss Maitland, please trust me. Shut your eyes and allow me to take your hand and lead you these last few steps."

Julia did as she was bid, and the touch of his hand in hers made her pulse race as he led her slowly forward and then stopped again.

"Now you may look."

Julia opened her eyes, expecting to see the sea. And she could, some way in the distance, perhaps two miles away. But what really caught her attention was what was in the foreground.

For there, about a hundred feet in front of her, was a ruined building built in the same golden yellow stone as Morancourt, glowing in the sunshine. On one side there was a circular building like a castle keep, with parts of the top broken and missing. Behind it, a line of lower outbuildings went in the direction of the sea.

On the other side, there was another substantial tall L-shaped building. To the left, she could see some damaged stained-glass windows with arched tops set in the lower part of the rougher stone wall and, on the right, there were straight walls pierced by arrow slits here and there. But between the keep and that building there was an arch, with a small central section missing. It was the *passerelle* that she had seen in the library picture at Morancourt.

Julia exclaimed with delight and turned to find him smiling at her with such a happy expression that it made her heart sing.

"Do you like the abbey, Julia?" he said.

And she had replied in the affirmative before she realised that he had used her Christian name and, from his expression, he had himself become aware of that at the same moment.

He took her hands in his, without saying anything, and then very gently took them up to his lips and kissed them, before releasing her fingers. Julia found herself almost overcome by the emotion that she felt at the pleasure of his touch, the urge to reciprocate, and his silent confirmation of how he felt about her. She could not trust herself to look at him, but stood by his side looking at the view and thinking her own thoughts for quite some time.

At last, when she was confident of some control over her voice, she ventured, "Can you tell me something of the history of the abbey?"

There was a pause before he replied, and Julia wondered if he, too, was finding it very difficult to control his emotions.

"A little. The site was originally occupied by an old castle—nothing grand, but a stronghold nevertheless—hence the circular keep. Later the site was given to an order of French monks, who came from Morancourt, and they extended the buildings to create their abbey, and lived happily enough here for two hundred years. But in the 1530s, King Henry the Eighth dissolved and closed all the monasteries, so that he could raise money from selling their buildings and land. Either that, or the abbey and the village were raided for slaves."

"Slaves?" exclaimed Julia.

"Yes. Pirates from northern Africa regularly raided coastal villages in northern Europe for many years—Spain, Portugal, France, Ireland, and other countries—to find white slaves to be taken back."

"I knew nothing of that."

"Many people have forgotten, but it is said that thousands of men and women were taken over the years from the coastal villages in Devon, Cornwall, and Dorset, and that the trade continued in some areas until the early part of this century."

"What would have happened to those unfortunate people?" said Julia, shivering at the thought.

"Some became labourers, perhaps in quarries, or building palaces for the rulers in cities such as Tunis. Or they were taken to be galley slaves, condemned never to set foot again on land, and the women were sought after as concubines. The wealthy amongst them were held for ransom. Whether the monks were taken as slaves, or whether the abbey was sold off by the King in the sixteenth century, local history does not say. But the monks did abandon the abbey here at Morancourt, and eventually the manor house was built further away from the coast, out of sight of the sea."

"When did the raids stop?"

"Much of the trouble came from Tunis, Tripoli, and Algiers, Algiers being the worst. That city was bombarded from the sea by our sailors in 1804 to try to stop the invasions. The American navy also assaulted the city, to prevent their ships that were trading with Europe from being boarded by the pirates. And many nations in Europe paid bribes to the North African rulers to call off their boats or seek their slaves elsewhere."

"I had no idea about such things!" exclaimed Julia.

"However, since Napoléon's blockade in the English Channel during the past few years, the invasions along the south coast have had a different character—smugglers—some call them free traders—bringing in contraband goods that cannot be obtained at present from Europe by any legal means."

He then led her by the hand underneath the arch to view the abbey from the other side and to look into several of the buildings that were more robust, and then out again to look down at the view of the coast and the sea.

"I do intend to renovate the manor house at Morancourt,

but my long-term plan is to live here in the abbey. It has, as you can see, the most wonderful view and there is a track to the village down there on the right, which could be improved to be the main access. My late godmother was very fond of this place, but she did not feel justified in spending very much money on it. I hope, one day, to live here with my family."

Julia did not reply; she was busy thinking how she would love to live in the abbey. If only she could persuade Mama that would be a much happier outcome than any marriage with Dominic Brandon.

Mr. Hatton broke into her thoughts. "Now, Miss Maitland, we could go back the way we came, or, if you prefer, we could turn left here and go through the woods, which you can see over there, where we would be more protected from this wind."

"Let's go through the trees," said Julia.

As they walked along a path towards the woods, the sun disappeared because a dark cloud was fast advancing on them from the sea.

"We are going to get wet, Mr. Hatton, but perhaps it will be less damp under some of the trees than if we were walking in the open."

"Yes," he replied, "but we must be glad that you have your pelisse, and I my cloak, as some protection."

As they had anticipated, they only walked for a short distance through the woods before the rain began to fall, first lightly as a shower, and then with increasing weight, until it was so torrential that they had to take shelter under a particularly dense tree. It was only when they had paused there for a short while that Mr. Hatton suddenly put his finger to his lips and said, very quietly, "Listen! Can you hear anything?"

Julia strained to see if she could discern a noise above the wind in the trees and the sound of the rain hitting the leaves. Yes, he was right, she could hear low voices, the sound of feet, and the rattle of something metallic.

Suddenly Mr. Hatton pulled her back behind the trunk of the tree, then between the shrubs in a hedge and below into a narrow ditch beyond. He pushed her down out of sight and laid next to her, spreading his black cloak over them both to conceal her light-coloured clothing. Then he clasped her close in the narrow space and whispered to Julia softly to be quiet, and she found herself shaking, though whether from fear or delight she could not tell.

The sounds were coming nearer now, and through the shrubs of the hedge she could see several dark figures moving steadily ahead along the path, some carrying boxes and others with pairs of tubs or barrels linked by lengths of wood bent by the weight of the contents into curves resting on their shoulders. One of the figures was carrying a metal box with a chain attached, which clanked as he walked along the track, with his boots squelching in the mud.

"Come on now, young Jem," said a voice in a local accent. "Stop making so much noise with that box, and just follow me as fast as you can."

There was a muttered reply that Julia could not make out as the figures passed just above where she and her companion were hiding, their feet making the leaves and twigs rustle on the track.

It seemed a long time to Julia before they had all passed, and the sounds began to recede into the distance. There must have been at least six men, perhaps ten, each carrying something heavy.

At last the rain eased and Mr. Hatton whispered in her ear, "I think that they have all gone, and we had better be on our way."

He helped her gently to get to her feet, and Julia brushed her dress clear of some of the leaves and most of the earth attached to her skirt. Then he took her arm and helped her up out of the ditch, through the hedge, and back onto the rough track.

Neither of them spoke for the first two hundred yards; they walked as silently as they could along the path until the trees in the woods began to give way to more open ground, and then they found themselves well below the ridge of the hill and looking down the slope towards the manor house at Morancourt.

"Who were they, Mr. Hatton? Smugglers?"

"Yes, I believe so. They were probably on the way to store the goods in the abbey, or in some of those farm buildings that we saw yesterday. It looks as though I will need to investigate what is going on here very soon. I won't be able to restore the abbey as I wish to if my land is infested with smugglers."

"May I help you?"

He paused and turned to look at her. "It might seem like an exciting adventure, Miss Maitland, but there is a lot of money involved in smuggling, and the last thing that I would want is to put you in any danger."

"The same applies to you, sir. Why is it that men always think that they have to do everything themselves?" She was only partly joking.

"Miss Maitland, of course I would like you to help me, but I would never forgive myself if any harm came to you."

"Unless you want me to call you Mr. Hatton forever, sir, you will have to treat me as an equal."

He looked at her steadily for quite a few moments, and then

said, "That must be the ultimate threat—if my father could hear you, he would have an even higher opinion of you than he already has."

This reply was so unexpected that Julia had to laugh. "Indeed, Mr. Hatton. We cannot possibly disappoint your father, or indeed me. So please may I help you investigate?"

"Very well, as long as you will listen to me when a situation seems to be getting too dangerous even for a spirited young lady from Derbyshire."

As she ran her fingers through her hair, Julia realised that she must be a very untidy sight. Mr. Hatton also looked dishevelled, with twigs clinging to his cloak and tendrils of his hair hanging down over his green eyes, and suddenly they both began to laugh at their situation.

Eventually Mr. Hatton said, "We had better walk back now, or your aunt will be wondering where we have got to."

When they entered the house, they tried to tidy themselves up in the hall before going into the salon to see her aunt. Mrs. Jones took their damp outer garments, and the footman went to fetch a change of shoes for both of them. However, Aunt Lucy had heard the noise, and was concerned to see how wet parts of their other clothing had become, as she had seen the downpour outside the windows. It took some conversation before they were able to calm her, and Julia concentrated on describing the delights of the old abbey and the pleasant views down towards the sea. Nothing was said about what she and Mr. Hatton had encountered in the wood.

"Have you heard, Julia, that James Lindsay is coming with his mother to visit us tomorrow morning? I am sure that your mama would approve of your meeting a baronet again!"

Julia gave her aunt what she intended to be a withering stare.

Mr. Hatton was not deceived by Aunt Lucy's remark, or by Julia's reaction. "Mrs. Harrison, I have had sufficient acquaintance with you to know that you intend Miss Maitland to bridle at that!"

Aunt Lucy smiled and then excused herself to take a short rest.

"As long as neither of you is serious," said Julia after her aunt had left the room. "Although he is quite the most pleasant baronet that I have met so far, in my limited acquaintance, I do not find myself with a personal partiality for your friend Sir James."

This idea did not seem to have occurred to Mr. Hatton, and he looked rather taken aback until he caught her expression and realised that she was joking with him in her turn.

"He does seem to me a very agreeable man, and I'm sure that my aunt would approve, but I suspect that he may not like my sometimes rather practical turn of mind."

"You judge him too severely, Miss Maitland. James does not have a narrow view of new farming practices, such as those used at Holkham Hall."

"How long has he been in charge of the family estate?"

"For about five years. He really had no choice, following the early death of his father, as he is the only son. I daresay that Lady Lindsay, who is a very competent person, could have kept the estate going for a while if James had decided to become an officer in Wellington's army. He used to talk of that when we were at school."

"So he might have chosen to serve with you in Spain?"

"Yes, that is true. He did discuss the possibility with me after his father's death but, bearing in mind the circumstances, he did not feel that he could lay that burden on his mother."

"What were those circumstances, Mr. Hatton?"

"His father volunteered to serve in Portugal when Wellington was short of experienced officers at the very beginning of the Peninsular Campaign. Sadly, Gervase Lindsay was killed by a sniper soon after he reached the conflict. He was only forty-five years old; James was away at school with me at the time. His two sisters, Anna and Helena, are younger, and he has no brothers. So James inherited the baronetcy, the house, and the land with it. With the help of a good steward and the farm manager, Lady Lindsay kept the estate going until he had enough experience to take charge."

War, thought Julia, exacts a heavy price wherever you look. How many families now had lost fathers, brothers, and sons, or seen them injured, all in the cause of the conflict against Napoléon?

꧁꧂

Lady Lindsay arrived promptly at the manor house on the following morning with her son and was introduced to Aunt Lucy, with whom she soon began an animated conversation in the salon. Mr. Hatton invited Julia and Sir James to join him in the library, where they could have some private conversation.

"Miss Maitland, please sit down," said Mr. Hatton.

Julia did as she was bid, then he continued. "Well, James, what have you been able to discover for me?"

"First, that my cousin Patrick has been in Bridport visiting his half brother, Frank, at least twice in the past month. On one of those occasions, he was accompanied by a friend from London, but I could not find out who he was. Second, that Frank Jepson has recently moved house again. It seems that he fell afoul of Isaac Gulliver by trespassing on his territory near Burton Bradstock. However, Jepson has since bought a sizeable property on the west side of Bridport, so he is obviously not short of money."

"Mr. Hatton, may I say something?"

He turned and looked at Julia with surprise, but it was Sir James who replied, "Of course, Miss Maitland, what is it?"

"Mrs. Harrison's personal maid, Martha Fisher, comes from near Bath. On the journey down here, she told us that her brother, Jem, had given up mining coal there in Radstock, and had travelled some months ago with other men to work in well-paid jobs near the coast."

Mr. Hatton was suddenly alert. "Jem, did you say?"

"Yes. You may remember that we heard that name mentioned when we were—we were walking in the wood." Julia turned her face away, knowing that she was blushing.

"Why is that important?" asked Sir James.

"A young man of that name, said to be a farmhand, was brought into Mrs. Jones's kitchen here at Morancourt the other day, having hurt his leg. By chance, I came across Mrs. Harrison's maid; she was very upset. Martha told me that it was her brother Jem Fisher, who had been working as a coal miner near Bath until recently."

"A miner should get much better pay than a farmhand, so why would he want to change jobs?"

"Martha told me that her brother had never worked as a farmhand, as far as she was aware."

"I wonder?" said Mr. Hatton. "Do you know where he is living now?"

"No, but Mrs. Jones said that her husband had brought him in to have the wound dressed. And she said that most of the farmhands lived in the village or in estate cottages."

"Something odd, Kit?" said Sir James. "Or just a coincidence, perhaps?"

"Let me think about it, and I will speak to Mr. Whitaker, for he will know the names of all the men that I employ on the estate. Miss Maitland, please do not do anything concerning this unless I say so. Frank Jepson has come to the attention of the authorities several times in the past, I understand, and I have been told that he has been known to use a weapon when crossed." He looked for confirmation at Sir James, who nodded in agreement.

Julia suddenly remembered what the mysterious man on Eggardon Hill had said, and felt sick.

"Come now, Miss Maitland, let us rejoin your aunt. I am sure that my mother would like to speak with you before we leave," and Sir James led the way back to the salon.

That afternoon, the sun was shining in a clear blue sky, and Mr. Hatton suggested that Julia should find her walking boots and a dark-coloured jacket, to walk with him past the Whitakers' farmhouse on the well-worn track that they had seen towards the sea. It took them about thirty minutes to reach the place where Mr. Hatton had paused the curricle previously.

"Now, Miss Maitland, shall we do a little exploring together? We will try to avoid the ditches this time! And we had better be circumspect about speaking too loudly."

Mr. Hatton led the way along the narrow path down towards the little valley, and round the slope of the ground until they could see the seashore some distance ahead of them. There were low cliffs on each side of the coast guarding what seemed to be a small bay. On the left of the track, the route they were following led to a gate in a low stone wall that encircled a group of stone barns with old thatched roofs.

"Do you think . . . ?" said Julia.

He anticipated her question. "Not being used for farming, I believe, as the worn track is too narrow for carts. Let us get a little closer, but remember to listen as we walk."

Nothing was heard, however, as they reached the barns and went through the gate to peer through a crack in one of the shuttered openings. Beyond, in the gloom, they could just make out stacked piles of small barrels and metal boxes on one side, and on the other some bales of fabric resting on a low table.

"We've seen enough," said Mr. Hatton. "I'll wager that those are all contraband goods, brought direct from the shore and made ready for moving on further inland when they can. Come back with me now, Miss Maitland, before anyone sees us here."

"Could we not go down to look at the coast before we return?"

He hesitated, then pointed to their right, where there was a band of trees beside the track. "Very well, but we will walk that way, not on the path, so that we are less visible."

As they advanced through the trees, the sound of the sea became audible at last, breaking on rocks along the coast below them. When they emerged from the wood, they found themselves still close to the track and on a slope overlooking the beach. There was no one in sight in either direction, although to the west the buildings on the coast at West Bay could just be seen in the far distance.

"What are those objects?" said Julia, pointing out to sea directly ahead.

Mr. Hatton looked carefully at the indistinct shapes breaking the surface of the water between the waves, and then replied, "James Lindsay is a local magistrate and he has told me that the smugglers sometimes need to keep their goods offshore until the revenue men have passed by. So what you can see may be markers or floats."

"For what, Mr. Hatton?"

"They sometimes sink casks of spirits, having put them on rafts or roped them together in groups, all attached to large stones. Then at night they can be pulled up to the surface of the water and taken to shore by small fishing boats like that one below us there."

Julia looked down onto the beach where he was pointing, and eventually she managed to glimpse a small fishing boat that had been pulled back from the water's edge and partly concealed between some rocks.

"Do they ever get caught by the revenue men?"

"Not often, as they can be out-numbered by the smugglers. Even if someone is caught, the jury of local people often acquit them. There is a lot of sympathy in Dorset for the smugglers, because the goods they bring in keep prices down, and would often not be available otherwise. Did you or Mrs. Harrison purchase any lengths of silk as gifts whilst you were staying in Bath?"

"Only one," she said, surprised, "for my mother."

"Well, that was probably smuggled into Dorset not far from here! Now, Miss Maitland, we had better not linger, just in case anyone thinks of coming by. Let us go back through the trees as far as we can, and then rejoin the track closer to the farmhouse."

On the walk back to the manor house, they discussed the various options open to Mr. Hatton, and concluded that he needed to make further inquiries now of Sir James, and anyone else who could be trusted not to disclose that the smuggling was being investigated.

When she descended the stairs the next morning, Julia was surprised to see that her aunt was not in her usual place for breakfast in the dining room, and found her walking slowly and steadily across the salon with Mrs. Jones and Martha in close attendance. Indeed, her aunt seemed anxious to venture out of doors for the first time.

"I do believe that I shall be well enough to travel home to Bath in a few days, Julia, perhaps on Monday. So, if there is anything else that you wish to do before we leave here, please do not delay in asking Mr. Hatton."

Julia's hidden reaction to this news was considerable dismay at the thought of leaving Morancourt and all that it had come to mean to her, and having so little time left with their host. But she replied quite calmly to her aunt.

"He did suggest that he could teach me to dance the waltz in the ballroom, Aunt Lucy, if you would agree to that."

Julia knew that, if the same question were to be addressed to Mama, the answer would be no, and that Aunt Lucy would be aware of that. But she also knew that Aunt Lucy shared some characteristics with her niece Sophie, and that she did not always choose to do exactly what people expected of her.

As Mr. Hatton came into the hall from his study to join them, Aunt Lucy replied, "I don't see why not, my dear, in a private setting such as this. Don't you agree, sir?"

When Mr. Hatton heard what Julia's question had been, he turned to her and said in a very level voice, "That is very good news, Miss Maitland." It was only when she saw the expression in his green eyes that she realised how much the answer meant to him.

TEN

The morning brought two letters from Derbyshire.

The first was for Julia and came from Emily at Cressborough Castle. She had been over to see Sophie and Harriet at Banford Hall, and she passed on all the gossip from the sisters. They were all looking forward to Julia's return, and Papa had asked for her to be told the same. Emily said that the Earl and Countess were in good health, and that they would all three be staying at the Castle for the next few weeks. Freddie had finally written a short note from Spain, to say that he was well but not looking forward to the colder weather, as the regiment was likely to be in the mountains over the winter. There was no mention of Dominic Brandon.

The second letter was from Mama for Aunt Lucy, full of pride at having achieved an invitation from the Earl and Countess for Julia and her aunt to stay at the Brandon's town house overnight on their forthcoming journey back to Banford Hall. There was no mention of Dominic Brandon in the letter, but seeing Julia's face fall at the suggestion of returning via London told her aunt what she had already guessed.

As Mrs. Jones was in the room with them at the time, all Aunt Lucy said was, "We can discuss our route to Derbyshire when we get back to Bath, my dear. I have suggested to Mr. Hatton that we leave here on Monday morning. He will escort us as far as Beaminster, and we will travel on from there."

Her aunt laid the letter down and picked up a book she had been reading, so Julia went up to her room and began to write a long reply to Emily. She recounted some information that she had heard about the local smuggling, but made no mention of Aunt Lucy's ankle.

Later that morning, Julia came across Mr. Hatton in the hall, and he asked her to join him in his study.

"I have spoken to Mr. Whitaker, Miss Maitland. There is no farmhand named Jem on the estate here as far as he is aware, nor have any of our labourers been injured recently. I have sworn him to secrecy about the matter, and it was rather odd, as somehow he seemed to be relieved at the news."

"Do you think that he suspects that something is going on somewhere on the estate, but he does not know what?"

"That's possible—he may not feel that he knows me well enough yet to trust me completely, but hopefully that will change soon."

Julia looked thoughtful, then said, "Do you think that Mr. Jones might be involved? He was born in this area and has been employed here for much longer than Mr. Whitaker, I imagine."

He looked startled for a moment. "Of course, you said that Mr. Jones had taken Jem into the kitchen for his wife to attend to the wound. So presumably Mr. Jones had either found him lying somewhere, or was with him when he was hurt?"

"Yes, one or the other."

"Hmm." He was drumming his fingers on the desk as Julia waited. "You did offer to help me, so could you ask his wife whether they, and in particular Mr. Jones, have any close friends in the village?"

"Very well," she replied. "After I have seen how Aunt Lucy is, I will look for her and ask the question."

Later Julia found Mrs. Jones upstairs, sorting the household linen.

"In case I do not have a better opportunity, Mrs. Jones, can I thank you now for being so kind to my aunt since her accident? It has been a great weight off my mind that she has had you to care for her and to call upon. And I have been able to make several excursions into the countryside around here knowing that she was in such good hands."

Mrs. Jones looked flustered but flattered at these remarks, and assured Julia that it had been a pleasure to be of assistance. From this, the conversation moved on to how long Mrs. Jones had been at Morancourt, where she had been born and brought up, and how she had met her husband.

"Mr. Jones was a soldier as a very young man," she told Julia, "but I met him after he came back from France about twenty years ago. There was a whole group of them who went to join the army from near here, for most could not find any employment in this area. He was lucky, for his father was already employed on this estate so, when Mr. Jones came back, he was offered a job by Mr. Henry Hatton. My husband did well, and ended up being in charge of the farm here."

"Does he mind not doing that anymore?"

"No, for it really needs a younger man in charge now—Mr. Henry Hatton bought more land later on, several years before he died, so there has been much more to do now than before. Mr. Jones is quite happy looking after the park, and he gets more time to meet his old friends from the army in the local public houses."

"It must be pleasant to keep in touch with friends from so long ago?"

"Yes. Some lads were killed or wounded of course, but others came home in one piece. A few married French girls whilst they were abroad, and brought them home when they had finished with the army. It must be odd having to leave all your family behind like that, though I suppose that the French girls were able to keep in touch with them before the Blockade."

"Oh, yes!" said Julia, "I had not thought of that. I know that some goods—silk for instance—are difficult to come by now because of the Blockade?"

"Yes, although it's surprising what you can get in Bridport if you really know where to look. One of the other men living in the village has a friend in that town, Frank, who has some very useful connections."

After some further conversation, Julia left her, and later went to tell Mr. Hatton what she had discovered.

"Mr. Jones had served in France, you say, Miss Maitland? That's interesting, and also other local people that he's known for a long time? And she mentioned someone called Frank? That could be Frank Jepson. And that was a clever idea of yours about the silk."

"I am sorry that I cannot be of more use," said Julia, "but I do not have much time left, and perhaps it would be unwise for my interest to be known."

"I agree, and there are other ways that information can be discovered."

How dull my life is going to be when I leave here, thought Julia.

"This is your last evening, Miss Maitland. May I introduce you to the waltz in the ballroom tonight?"

"Certainly, sir, although I have no means of knowing how long it will take me to become proficient. Would you say that you are a competent teacher?"

He threw back his head and laughed. "Probably not, Miss Maitland, with my limp restricting my agility, but I hope that between us we shall do very well!"

Julia then remembered something that she had wanted to ask him.

"Would you mind if I try to make a copy, however amateurish, of the picture in your library? It would be a pleasure for me to have it when I am back in Derbyshire and," she hesitated, "be a happy memento of a very pleasant stay here at Morancourt." She nearly added, "with you," but she suddenly felt so emotional that she feared she might burst into tears.

"Oh! Of course you may do so if you wish."

"Thank you. I have been so busy enjoying myself that I have not had time to use the small box of paints and the few sheets of watercolour paper that I brought with me from Bath."

Julia turned and, without saying any more, went up the stairs to fetch them.

It was some two hours later that Aunt Lucy came to find her. "Julia, I have been searching for you all over the house. Fortunately, I learnt that Mr. Hatton knew where you were. How is your painting?"

Julia rose from the seat at the table she had been using, allowing her aunt to see what she had been doing. The watercolour was not a bad copy of the painting on the wall, and at the bottom Julia had just written "*La Passerelle.*"

"What does that mean, my dear?"

"It is a nickname, but I suppose that you could otherwise call it 'Paradise.'"

Her aunt, surprised, looked from the painting to her niece without saying anything, but she put her arm around Julia's shoulders for a few moments and held her tightly.

Then Aunt Lucy said, "It is nearly time to dress for dinner, my dear," before she turned away and left the room.

Julia looked out of the window of the library for a few minutes without seeing anything. Then she put her painting materials into the box and closed the lid, rolled up her copy of the picture, and hurried to take everything back upstairs.

Mrs. Jones and the cook had clearly decided to surpass themselves in preparing the dishes on the menu for dinner. They had even, Julia discovered, prepared one of the desserts using the lemons that Julia had bought in Beaminster.

"I suppose," said Mr. Hatton, "that this is the Derbyshire pudding that you mentioned to me the other day?"

"Of course, sir," said Julia with an equally enigmatic expression.

Aunt Lucy clearly enjoyed this repartee, and the rest of the meal. She was looking fully restored to health, and dinner passed with many happy exchanges of views.

At nine o'clock, Aunt Lucy rose from her chair and said firmly, "Now my dears, I am going to my room to finish the packing with Martha. In particular, I shall be wrapping the miniature rocking horse very carefully as a happy memento of my dear friend Susannah. Thank you again for letting me have that gift, Mr. Hatton."

He bowed his head to her briefly in acknowledgment.

"I shall not be coming downstairs again until tomorrow morning. But I do expect to hear that Julia has become an expert at the waltz when I see you both then, Christopher."

Mr. Hatton and Julia rose to their feet and wished her good

night as she left the room. For a short while, there was an awkward silence.

Then he said, "Miss Maitland, am I right in saying that Mrs. Harrison used my Christian name to give me permission to use yours?"

"Yes, I suppose that you must be right, for I have never heard her call you that before."

"Then please come with me now, Julia."

And he walked from the end of the room around the side of the dining table and held his hand out to her. When she offered hers in return, he clasped it firmly, and they went through the house, pushed the stiff doors open, and entered the ballroom.

There, to her surprise, Julia found that there were four groups of candelabra with the candles already lit. The curtains had been drawn against the night, and the drabness of the decorations did not seem to matter as much as they had before.

"First," he said, "please stand back over there and I will try to give you a demonstration of my part in the dance."

Julia stood still at the side of the ballroom, and Mr. Hatton began to hum to himself.

"It is a tempo, like this—ONE, two, three. ONE, two, three. ONE, two, three. ONE, two, three. ONE, two, three." After he had established the rhythm, he began to move his feet in time, holding his arms out to an imaginary partner, turning his body and crossing the length of the ballroom as he did so, back and forth.

"You are not meant to take this too seriously, Julia!"

As she had been smiling at him since he began to hum the tune, she did not have much difficulty with that.

"ONE, two, three. ONE, two, three. ONE, two, three. ONE, two, three. ONE, two, three," he continued for a few minutes more.

"Now, Julia, for your part. The ladies have to echo, reflect, the same steps but whilst moving backwards, and facing their partner. That must be more difficult, I suppose? Try it first on your own."

Julia began to move slowly across the ballroom, humming the tune as she did so, "ONE, two, three. ONE, two, three. ONE, two, three. ONE, two, three. ONE, two, three."

He smiled at her encouragingly.

Julia then went back in the opposite direction, repeating the tune as she went, "ONE, two, three. ONE, two, three. ONE, two, three. ONE, two, three. ONE, two, three."

"Bravo!" he exclaimed. "Well done, Julia."

The sound of her name on his lips gave her such a warm feeling that Julia was able to reply, without any constraint in her voice, "Thank you, Kit. Now what next?"

"Now we must dance the two parts together. You put your hand on my shoulder, and I have my arm around your waist—like this." And he came towards her, indicating that she should lift her right hand onto his shoulder, then he put his left hand round her waist, and with his other hand clasped her free hand.

The feeling of being so close to him made her feel—she could not have described it in words—there was a warmth, an excitement, a trembling feeling within her that she had never felt before. He said nothing, but he held her hand even more tightly, which made her sure that he felt the same.

After a little while, he cleared his throat and said, "Now, Julia, we must move together. That is, I mean, in the same direction."

She realised that he was trying to make a joke, and to make some sense of how he was feeling as he began the tune again.

"Now, let us begin. ONE, two, three. ONE, two, three. ONE, two, three. ONE, two, three. ONE, two, three."

After an unsteady start, they began to move together as one around the room, from the end by the tall windows to the other, where a tall mirror hung above the stone fireplace. Just occasionally, his slight limp impeded them. Julia could see them both in a reflection in the mirror, looking over Kit's shoulder at their image as they turned and moved as one. She could not have said how long it was before they stopped, nor would she have cared if the ballroom had been full of people instead of just the two of them—the couple in the mirror.

At last they came to rest, but he did not release her. Instead, he gently took his right hand from her left and held her head against his shoulder.

"Julia," he breathed, "we must, we have to, find a way to be together forever."

She could think of nothing useful to say, nor wished to lift her head from his shoulder, storing the memory in her mind so that she might never lose it.

Finally he let her go from his embrace and held her at arms' length, waiting until she could meet his eyes.

"Julia." He stopped and could not go on, his voice thick with emotion.

She found the strength to speak. "Kit, we will, I am sure we will somehow. Please, please, don't make me cry. I am so happy, and this can't be the end of the story."

For a moment, she thought that he was going to take her in his arms again. But after a short step towards her, he steadied himself and said, "No, I cannot risk it. I may not be able to control myself, and that is not what I want to happen tonight. Julia, we must go now to the bottom of the stairs, and say good night as we normally do."

Then he held out both his hands to her, and when she put her hands in his, he lifted her fingers to his lips and kissed them once before letting them drop and then leading her to the foot of the stairs.

There he said formally, "Good night, Miss Maitland, and thank you."

Julia afterwards could not remember how she replied before curtseying to him and turning to go up the stairs.

The next morning, all was hustle and bustle as their trunks were loaded onto the carriage, and the various farewells said to Mrs. Jones and her staff.

If Aunt Lucy was observing them carefully, she did not show it, but said good-bye formally to "Mr. Hatton" before getting into the carriage. Julia and Martha followed her, the coachman took up the reins as Mr. Hatton mounted his horse, and they started down the drive. Most of the time, the road back to Beaminster was too narrow for him to ride beside them but, once they reached the town, the travelling chaise paused in the square, and Aunt Lucy said, "Martha, please go now, and make a small purchase of that Blue Vinney cheese for us to take home to Bath."

To Julia she said, "Get out of the carriage for a few moments, my dear, and say good-bye to Mr. Hatton."

Julia did as she was told, and Mr. Hatton dismounted and gave the reins of his horse to the coachman to hold. They walked away from the carriage for a few steps, and then stood together on the cobbled sideway.

Suddenly, something that had been niggling at the back of her mind came to Julia, and she said, "Mr. Hatton, can you please ask Sir James to find out the name inscribed in the church register for the christening of Frank Jepson? And then can you please write to me or to my aunt at Banford Hall to let me know the answer?"

Whatever he had thought she was going to say, it was not that, and all he could reply was "Why, Miss Maitland?"

"Because Sir James said that he was illegitimate."

He looked at her blankly, and then comprehension dawned. "So the surname recorded should not have been his father's?"

"Yes, exactly."

He smiled at her warmly, and then said out loud, "What a pleasure it is to know someone with such an inquiring mind." Then he leant forward and whispered in her ear, "Good-bye, dearest Julia. We shall meet again, never fear, and all will be well."

She smiled at him, wordless and now almost in tears, before he squeezed her hands briefly, and she got back into the carriage next to her aunt. Once Martha had returned with her purchase, the coach was soon on its way out of the square, and she could not bear to look to see him getting smaller in the distance.

Very little was said between them on the way back to Bath. The constraint of Martha's presence did not allow for any personal conversation, and Aunt Lucy seemed intent on observing the scenery passing by the carriage window. Julia's mind was full of many thoughts. Although they must have stopped at an inn for the night, in retrospect she had no recollection of its location. Sufficient to say that it was on the second day in the afternoon that the coachman gathered his horses and held them back as they drove down the long hill at Holloway into Bath.

Julia found it odd to be back in her aunt's house in the city without Emily being there. It was not that Julia minded the house being much quieter, but her friend's lively presence had been a constant entertainment. Before they went to bed that night, her aunt said, "Tomorrow, Julia, we will discuss how we will occupy ourselves. I am planning to leave for Derbyshire in about six days' time. Now try and get a good night's sleep, my dear."

Julia had not realised how tired she was, and Martha did not wake her the following morning until about ten o'clock. Aunt Lucy had finished her breakfast by the time her niece descended the stairs and was sitting in the drawing room reading another letter from her sister, Olivia, Julia's mother.

"I should tell you, Julia, that I have no intention of taking Olivia's advice to travel back through London. You can tell me more in the next day or two about this Dominic Brandon, but it is much more important for you to get home in a happy frame of mind to see your father."

Julia's immediate reaction was that her mother would be very angry at this news, but Aunt Lucy had already thought that through.

"I will leave writing to tell your mother for a day or two. I suggest that you might like to send a letter at the same time, to thank the Earl and Countess for their kind offer of accommodation in London. But you have my authority to say to them that I was adamant that we should travel back north through the city of Oxford and Market Harborough."

"I had guessed," said Julia, "that you understood many things that I have not been able to explain, and I'm very grateful for that. Thank you. I should be very glad to have a talk with you before I leave Bath."

She embraced her aunt, and at her suggestion went to her room to find one of the books from the library that she had not yet finished reading.

Together, they settled into a gentle routine during the next few days. Although Julia had enjoyed Emily's company very much and the busy social round during her previous stay in Bath, she was glad of the opportunity to see more of the city's character during this second visit. Aunt Lucy did not suggest attending concerts or going to balls. Instead they walked around the centre and along the handsome terraces of houses that lined the streets. They had a pleasant wander up and down Milsom Street looking at the shops, sometimes eating a cake at a table in Mollands' pastry shop, varied by a visit to the Pump Room to take the waters. Then they made a diversion into the lending library in the Orange Grove, and visited the shops nearby, where they chose some more gifts for Julia to take home to her family.

On a sunny morning, Aunt Lucy took her niece with her to walk across the fields below the famous Royal Crescent, where the terrace of thirty houses formed a most impressive curve overlooking the green sward which ran down towards the river bank. There was a constant procession of fashionable people walking to and fro on the grass, meeting and greeting their friends as they went.

On the way home, towards the centre of town, they were passed by a sedan chair, with the two chairmen labouring under the weight of a rather large gentleman.

"That man," said Aunt Lucy, "would be better to walk back into the city, rather than ride and give those poor chairmen such a heavy load to carry!"

Julia agreed and was about to ask how much it cost to hire a chair when her aunt surprised her.

"I have made an appointment for you this afternoon, Julia, with one of the best dancing masters from London, Mr. Thomas Wilson. He is said to be the most expert teacher available in Bath with a knowledge of the waltz, and I thought that you might like to improve your skills."

This remark brought Mr. Hatton firmly back into Julia's

mind, and the memory of that happy evening when they had crossed and crisscrossed the floor in his ballroom at Morancourt, if not always in step together, at least of one mind.

"Oh, dear aunt, how kind you are, thank you!"

Back at Aunt Lucy's house, Julia went looking for Martha to help tidy her hair, but could not find her anywhere. Coming down the stairs from her bedroom, Julia came across her aunt and asked whether she had seen Martha.

"No, my dear, for she's not here in Bath at present. I have given her a few days' holiday, and she has gone to stay with her elder sister in that village near Gloucester. Martha will be back here in the city next week."

"But will you not want her to go with you to Derbyshire?"

"No, I shall be taking Eliza instead, one of the housemaids who has helped me before when Martha has been unwell. That seems a much better course, so that Martha has no opportunity to gossip with your parents' servants in Derbyshire about our stay at Morancourt."

Julia had not thought of that and expressed her gratitude for her aunt's careful anticipation.

That afternoon, Julia attended at the rooms of Mr. Thomas Wilson, where she and several other young ladies practiced their skills in dancing the waltz, accompanied by a small group of local musicians playing the tunes. After two hours of having her every move adjusted to the satisfaction of the dancing master, Julia was technically much more proficient. However, as she reflected to herself during the walk back to her aunt's house with the maid Eliza, she had had much more enjoyment dancing that one evening in Dorset.

It was on the next day, when they were sitting together in the drawing room drinking a cup of tea, that Aunt Lucy said at last, "Now Julia, tell me something about this Dominic Brandon, and that other suitor that your mother does not seem to like very much."

Julia did not have much difficulty with the first part of this request, although she left out some of the wilder details of Lord Brandon's life in London.

"Please understand me, dear aunt. Dominic and his parents are not unpleasant people, and Mama is quite right in saying that I would never want for anything—dresses, money, jewels—if I were to marry him. But I would never be happy, or feel that I was the most important person in his life. To be the next Countess of Cressborough would be no recompense for that as far as I am concerned."

Her aunt nodded but kept silent, so Julia continued. This, she knew, was going to be the more difficult bit to explain. Over the past two days, she had realised that she had to tell Aunt Lucy sometime soon that Kit Douglas and Mr. Hatton were one and the same.

She started with a short description of her first visit to Norton Place to meet Jack Douglas, and her reaction to him, to his younger brother, and to their father. She did not want to mention the gift of the red shoes, but she was able to suggest that there had been from the beginning some mutual interest between her and Kit Douglas.

"But I assume," said Aunt Lucy, "that you saw no future in that, as he was the younger son?"

"No, you are right. Papa said the same, and of course I am not stupid. I do understand why."

"So that is one reason why your father suggested that you should come and stay with me in Bath?"

"Yes, and I was very grateful for the invitation, and you were so kind in suggesting that Emily could join me. But then something happened after I arrived in Bath that I am ashamed of—that is, I mean that I deliberately deceived you."

Her aunt's expression changed, but not to annoyance, only to curiosity.

Julia then explained her emotions when Mr. Hatton had been announced in Aunt Lucy's drawing room for the first time, of how Kit Douglas had suggested that their previous acquaintance should not be revealed and why.

"You will perhaps understand, dear aunt, why to begin with I did not want to go to Dorset. It meant that I was going to have to maintain that lie, but in the end I could not help myself, the opportunity to see more of Kit, I mean Mr. Hatton, was something that I could not give up. Then there was the unfortunate injury to your ankle, which led to two things. First, that our stay at Morancourt was to be extended—you can imagine that I was not at all unhappy about that. But second, that I continued to deceive you, which I very much regretted. I suppose at that point I could have told you the truth, and perhaps I should have done. But it is too late to alter that now."

Julia had been watching her aunt's expression as she spoke, and was not at all sure what her response was likely to be. But she need not have worried.

"Perhaps I should be angry, Julia, or at least a little annoyed at your deception. But if someone as worthwhile as Mr. Hatton wanted to marry me—and that's so, isn't it, my dear?—then I would have done the same. Unfortunately, your mother seems set on this other marriage, so that she can become the mother-in-law to an earl. We shall see what happens about that. Meanwhile, you have not said much about Mr. Harry Douglas, your father's friend. Does he know anything about all this?"

Julia repeated what Mr. Hatton had told her at Morancourt, that Mr. Douglas did not yet know of his son's inheritance, but that he would be told soon when he travelled to stay in Dorset.

"Would Mr. Douglas object, do you think, to Jack's being replaced in your affections by his brother? Perhaps I have put that badly, Julia, since Jack never seems to have been the subject of your interest to begin with."

"No! If anyone preferred Jack, it would be my sister Sophie, although they seem to have some unfortunate characteristics in common that would indicate that an alliance would not be a good idea. I liked Harry Douglas very much when we met, and I doubt whether he would object to my marrying Kit. But I dare not make any assumptions about that."

Her aunt then moved on to another subject.

"How many other people know that Kit Douglas and Mr. Hatton are the same person? Sir James Lindsay, his mother and his aunt certainly, and I suppose some of their servants. Also the servants at Morancourt, or some of them. I suppose that's all?" said Aunt Lucy.

Julia replied, "Sophie and Papa only met Kit at Norton Place. Emily Brandon has met Mr. Hatton, but not Kit Douglas, and Harriet has been away at school."

"And your mama?"

"She knows about Kit Douglas through my father, but as far as I'm aware she has not met him."

"Very well," said Aunt Lucy. "Then for the moment we need not worry about any news getting out in Derbyshire. Is there anything else that you should be telling me now, Julia? I did hear a hint, although not from you or Mr. Hatton, that smugglers might be active in some of the farm buildings at Morancourt."

This last remark, coming without any warning, stunned Julia. She gathered her wits, and then just simply replied that it was something that Mr. Hatton was looking into. She could tell, from her aunt's expression, that Aunt Lucy was not entirely convinced that her niece had told her everything on that subject, but her aunt did not pursue the matter.

That afternoon, when Julia returned with Eliza from visiting Milsom Street to make some last-minute purchases, she found that a letter had come for her from her youngest sister, Harriet. Julia took the letter into the drawing room before opening the seal and reading the contents. Her aunt could tell from her expression that the news was not good.

"What is it, my dear?" said Aunt Lucy gently, watching as her niece's face changed. "Is it your father?"

"Yes," said Julia, fighting back the tears. "Harriet says that he has now taken to his bed the whole time on the doctor's advice, and is having difficulty breathing steadily."

Her aunt did not try to console her by suggesting that things might not be as bad as Julia might imagine. Instead, she sent for Eliza and told her to start collecting their clothes, ready to pack for the journey.

"But, Julia, we are not going to leave until the day after tomorrow, however anxious you are. One day's delay will make very little difference. I need to write to your mama, and you to the Earl and Countess at Cressborough Castle, telling them that our return journey will not be via the town house in London, and that we hope to be back at Banford Hall by the end of this week."

"Very well, Aunt."

"My letter will not give your mother enough time to do anything to spoil my plans," said Aunt Lucy.

And what could only be described as a very wicked smile came over her aunt's face. Julia recognised that expression, for it was familiar—it was the kind of smile that an elder sister uses when she has triumphed over a younger sibling.

ELEVEN

Despite her regrets at leaving Bath, Julia enjoyed the journey home with Aunt Lucy and Eliza. They stopped for the first night in Oxford, staying at a comfortable inn. The college and university buildings were very handsome, and Julia imagined that Kit would have enjoyed studying in the city, if he had thought that it would be worthwhile for his chosen career. But, she reflected, if he had done so, they might never have met.

With the sun shining brightly, they took the chance to walk around the city for a couple of hours on the following morning before rejoining Eliza and taking their places in the carriage. Then they travelled on through the English Midlands, a long and dusty journey, before stopping again in the town of Market Harborough for the second night. On the last day, the scenery became more familiar, and eventually the chaise made the slow journey through the busy streets in the centre of Derby and then on for the last few miles towards Banford Hall.

The sound of the wheels on the gravel forecourt brought Sophie and Harriet to the front door. Aunt Lucy and her niece had difficulty in emerging from the carriage before they were enveloped in happy embraces, and they had to try to get inside the house before imparting all their news.

"How is Papa?" was Julia's first inquiry. Sophie was busy talking to Aunt Lucy, so it was Harriet who answered.

"You will see for yourself. He is resting at present, so let's wake him with some tea in about half an hour."

"Where is your mama?" asked Aunt Lucy.

The two younger sisters hesitated and looked at each other. Then Sophie said, "She has gone to shop in Bakewell and will be back later this afternoon."

Aunt Lucy and Julia exchanged looks—that meant that Mama was really displeased if she had deliberately absented herself when she had known that they were due to arrive. However, in the excitement of unpacking the trunks and exchanging other news, Julia did not have time to worry, and soon it was time to go to see Papa in his dressing room, where a bed had been set up so that he could see the view over to the dales from the first-floor window.

He opened his arms to Julia with a wonderful smile of welcome, although she could see that he had lost more weight, and he had difficulty in lifting his shoulders from the pillows.

"Julia, my dear, how well you look! Lucy, thank you for caring for her so well. You must both come and sit by me now and tell me all the news."

They did as he asked, and Julia gave a lively description of the activities in Bath. Emily had already told Sophie and Harriet about the expedition on the canal, but they were eager to hear it all again, as well as the details of life in the fashionable city at the height of the season.

"And what about your visit to Dorset, Lucy?" said Papa.

Julia was glad to have Aunt Lucy answer for her on that subject. She was intrigued to note how her aunt's account made no mention at all of her injured ankle. Although there was no deliberate deception, Aunt Lucy's description of what Julia had seen and done was told in such a way that it appeared that the two of them had experienced everything together. When Sophie asked her aunt to describe Mr. Hatton, she spoke of a pleasant man glad to assume his new responsibilities.

Sophie persisted in asking Julia, "And what did you think of him? Is he of marriageable age?"

"Yes, I suppose so, but he is definitely not your type, Sophie, and Dorset is a very long way from here!"

To her relief, that topic was not taken any further. In a while, more wheels could be heard on the gravel below the window, and Mama swept in, all graciousness in greeting her sister and, less so, her eldest daughter.

Aunt Lucy had brought a special gift for Mama, but mentioned it as though it had been entirely Julia's idea instead of the choice being shared between them. "Show your mother now, my dear."

Julia went to fetch the carefully wrapped package, which they had purchased in Milsom Street in Bath. Even Mama had to exclaim with pleasure when she saw the dress length of blue silk shot through with gold threads.

"Thank you both, my dears! How grand I shall be."

That evening, Aunt Lucy said firmly to her nieces, "I want to have a quiet discussion with my sister, Olivia, about your father, so why don't you all go up to Julia's room together? I'm sure that you have a lot to talk about."

Upstairs, Julia said to Sophie and Harriet, "Mama looks very worn."

"Yes, she is very unhappy that the doctor cannot do any more to help Papa," said Harriet. "We asked Emily Brandon if she knew of anyone else who could be consulted in Derby, and she asked the Countess. But apparently the local doctor is the best available in the county. And we asked Mr. Douglas as well, when he came."

"Oh! Has he been here recently to visit Papa?"

"Yes, Mr. Douglas came to Banford Hall a few days ago, to see Papa and to tell us that he would be away down south for a while visiting his younger son. He asked to be remembered to you, Julia."

"Is Emily coming here soon?"

"Yes, the day after tomorrow," said Harriet, "and she hopes to have some news of Freddie."

Sophie interrupted, "Has Mama said anything to you, Julia, about not coming back through London or staying at the Brandons' town house? She was so thrilled when Emily said that the Earl and Countess had offered that chance to you, and very angry indeed when she got Aunt Lucy's letter."

"No," said Julia, "but our aunt had already made up her mind by then about what route she wanted to use. I wrote to thank the Earl and Countess for their offer, and I'm sure that they would not really have minded. I didn't meet Dominic Brandon on my way to Bath through London, so it probably would not have been any different on the way back if we had come back through town."

After the others had left her, Julia took her watercolour picture of La Passerelle out of the bottom of her trunk, unrolled the paper, and pinned it up inside her clothes cupboard, where she would see it every time that she opened the door.

She was about to get ready for bed when there was a knock on the door. Julia had grown so accustomed to her aunt saying good night to her that it came as a surprise that the door opened and Mama came into the room.

As always with her mother, there were few preliminaries.

"You will not be surprised to know, Julia, that I was very unhappy indeed to learn that you did not visit the Brandons' town house on your way home," she said in her determined way. "Your aunt's explanation did not seem to me to justify the disrespect to a family who wishes you to marry their elder son."

Julia sought to speak, but was ignored.

"You will have already realised how much your father's health has deteriorated over the past few weeks, and it is imperative that the alliance with Lord Brandon be concluded as soon as possible. With help from Emily, we have an appointment at Cressborough Castle tomorrow morning, to meet the Earl and Countess. Please make sure that you are at the front door at nine o'clock, ready to leave."

And with that, she swept out, without waiting for any comment from her eldest daughter.

Julia was very tired after the long day travelling, and was longing to fall asleep as soon as her head touched the pillow. Instead, she lay there fuming at her mother's total disregard of her own wishes. She concocted various plans to avoid visiting the castle the next day, only to discard them as unrealistic and unlikely to succeed. Eventually she fell asleep and dreamt of chasing smugglers through the woods at Morancourt with Kit Hatton. When she woke with a start, it was already eight o'clock, and she had to hurry to be ready in time.

There was very little conversation between Julia and Mama on the journey to the castle, and the discomfort of travelling in their old coach on a rather dull morning was in stark contrast to the pleasant journey that she had made several weeks earlier with her father in the Brandons' barouche.

And it proved to be a rather confusing visit once they arrived at the castle.

The welcome they received was very similar to before, with the Earl and Countess awaiting them in the drawing room, but there was no sign anywhere of Dominic Brandon, much to her mother's dismay. Instead, Emily was sitting on the chaise longue close to her uncle and aunt.

"Julia, my dear, how are you?" said the Countess. "You look very well, and Emily has told me all about her stay with you and Mrs. Harrison in Bath, and what she knows about your visit with your aunt to Dorset."

Julia's quick glance at her friend reassured her that no confidences would have been passed on about the latter, but there was something in Emily's expression that cheered her. And so it proved.

"I must apologise most profusely, Mrs. Maitland," said the Earl, "but it seems that our elder son has been detained in town. He had promised us that he would be here to meet you in Derbyshire today, but that has apparently not proved to be possible."

Behind his back, Julia could see Emily silently mouthing the word "Christina" to her.

Her mama's disappointment could be heard in her voice (Mama is not a good liar, thought Julia), as she replied, "Please do not trouble yourself, my lord. It is just that my husband's ill health . . ." She stopped, and did not go on.

"I quite understand," said the Countess quietly, "and we will ask you to visit again as soon as Dominic arrives. We have sent urgent messages to town, and hope that Julia may soon be able to meet him here."

At this point, Emily asked her uncle and aunt if Julia could be spared for a few minutes to look at a new gown that she had acquired. The two young ladies sped away to the family's private rooms, where Emily produced the dress as promised, but indicated that it had really been a ruse to speak to Julia privately.

"Freddie's regiment has unexpectedly returned from the Peninsula. Dominic has not been seen at the house in town for several days, and Freddie guesses that he is with Christina. He also says that, during the past week, several acquaintances have called in search of my cousin. Apparently he has not been seen in any of his usual haunts for some time."

"Did his friends say what they wanted?"

"Some did, saying that Dominic had borrowed money from them that was now overdue for repayment, and another was looking to collect some 'fine goods from Dorset' as he put it."

"Oh!" said Julia. "That sounds like contraband. Did Freddie take any note of who these people were?"

"Yes, some of them, including the one waiting for the fine goods. We had better go back to the drawing room now, but I thought that you ought to know."

Emily and Julia went back to join the others and, after a further exchange of pleasantries and some light refreshments, Mrs. Maitland and her daughter took their leave and began the return journey.

Julia was disinclined to talk, but her mother spent much of the time before they reached Banford Hall regretting their wasted visit and urging Julia to keep her informed of any news that Emily might convey about her cousin's return to his ancestral home.

Julia had forgotten how lively it was sharing a house with her younger sisters, and she was glad that Papa's dressing room was tucked away at one end of the house so that they did not have to worry about disturbing him. It proved quite difficult to find an opportunity to speak to him privately. However, Aunt Lucy had brought with her a magazine showing the latest London fashions, and she persuaded Sophie and Harriet to join Mama in the drawing room so that they could all examine it.

Julia then went to the dressing room and found her father, as always, happy to talk to her.

"Did you enjoy your stay in Bath, and then in Dorset?"

"Oh, yes, Papa, you were quite right. I really needed a break from Derbyshire, although it would have been so much nicer if you could have been there as well. But I did my best to enjoy myself, and I had great fun with Emily in Bath. And when we went to Dorset, Aunt Lucy was very kind to me, and Mr. Hatton was a very civil host."

Her father asked her to describe the house at Morancourt, and he liked her account of its condition and furnishings, and the surrounding countryside. She mentioned the ruined abbey, and the view to the sea, and told him about Sir James Lindsay and their visit to his house. She hinted a little at the possibility of there being smuggling in the area, and this did not seem to worry him as much as it would have done her mama.

In reply to her question about his health, he looked rather more serious and said, "Julia, I have not told your mother, and I have asked the doctor to say very little to her. There is really no easy way to tell you, but he has warned me that I may not be here this time next year."

At this news, tears welled into her eyes, and Julia tried to turn her face away.

"No, my dear—please do not upset yourself too much, for there seems to be nothing at all that we can do about it. But, as the eldest in the family now, I feel that you should not be kept in the dark, as we may need to make financial plans for when the family can no longer live at Banford Hall."

Julia could not think of anything to say to this and put her arm around him, trying to put her strength into his weak frame.

When she had left him to have his rest, she found Aunt Lucy alone in the hall, opening a letter. After she had read it through, she turned to Julia.

"This is from Mr. Hatton, in reply to my note of thanks that I sent from Bath. He asks me to pass on a message from Sir James and says that you will know what it means. He says that the name that you wanted is François Jepson Labonne, and that his mother lived locally in Dorset at the time of his birth, but that she came from northern France. Do you understand all that, Julia?"

"Yes, thank you, dear aunt. That is exactly what I need to know."

"I must admit that I am consumed with curiosity."

"Forgive me, Aunt Lucy. I need to speak to Emily when she comes tomorrow before I can tell you anything more. It might be very useful if you could persuade Mama to go with you to Derby with my sisters, to choose a design for her silk dress at the dressmakers there."

"Very well, as long as you promise to let me in on the secret before too long."

Her aunt then asked Julia what had happened during the visit to Cressborough Castle, as her sister had clearly been dissatisfied with the outcome. Julia gave her a short account of what had happened, and Aunt Lucy said, "Very good, a few more days' delay may be helpful."

Aunt Lucy was as good as her word and, when Emily Brandon arrived the following morning, she had already left with Mama, Sophie, and Harriet in her chaise for the visit to Derby.

Julia and Emily spent the next hour catching up with all the news from Derbyshire and from Freddie. Dominic had not been back to Cressborough Castle since Julia had seen him there. Emily was anxious to hear more about what Julia had done in Dorset, and her friend told her as much as she could without revealing anything about her relationship with Mr. Hatton. But she did explain that there seemed to be a problem on the estate with contraband goods being brought onshore and hidden in farm buildings, before they were being sold to eager purchasers further inland.

Then Julia explained that one of the people suspected of being a ringleader in the smuggling ring was Frank Jepson—christened François Jepson Labonne.

"Labonne!" said Emily, startled. "But that is the same surname as Annette, the Countess's abigail. Do you remember that we saw Annette in Bath talking to Dominic and his friend Mr. Jepson—Jepson! But that is the same name as the smuggler?"

"Yes, and I saw Patrick Jepson in the square at Beaminster, the small town near Morancourt, a few days before we left there to go back to Bath, talking to the man called Frank Jepson."

"So," said Emily slowly, "we have two Mr. Jepsons, both seen in Dorset and one in Bath. At least one of them knows my cousin Dominic. And one had a French mother with the surname Labonne, the same as Annette?"

"Yes, and Sir James Lindsay, who was at school with Mr. Hatton, told him that Frank Jepson is the illegitimate elder brother of Patrick Jepson, his mother's nephew. So I wondered, Emily, whether there is any way that you could confirm whether Annette is really closely related to Frank Jepson. And rather than ask Annette directly, would it be worth speaking to the Countess herself?"

Emily considered this for a few moments. "Yes, that is the

best idea. I will not mention Dominic, or the smuggling ring. I do know that Annette has worked for the family for many years, since my cousins were very young, but the Countess may know where she lived before then."

"Is the Countess still at the castle?"

Emily nodded. "I think perhaps that I will not stay today for as long as I had planned. I really must find out what she knows about Annette."

"Then just stay to take a cup of tea with Papa, for he enjoys having visitors he knows well."

Papa was glad to see Emily and was entertained by the lively conversation between the two girls before she left. When the party returned from Derby in Aunt Lucy's travelling chaise, Sophie and Harriet were disappointed to hear that Emily had already gone home, but were mollified by Julia's confirming that their friend would be back soon.

Aunt Lucy persuaded all her nieces to go with her during the next few days to Buxton and Bakewell, and to visit Chatsworth, one of the largest stately homes in the locality. These excursions kept Julia's mind occupied, although her thoughts often strayed to Mr. Hatton in Dorset and, although less often, to Emily, hoping that she would be able to add a piece to the puzzle about Dominic.

Eventually the message came from the castle that Emily would be visiting Banford Hall that afternoon and, even better, that she would be bringing Freddie with her.

Whilst he regaled her younger sisters with news about his regiment's sudden return from Spain for the rest of the winter, Julia took her friend up to her room, where Emily lost no time.

"The Countess has told me that Annette has an older sister who met and married an English soldier while he was serving in France. When they returned to his home county of Dorset, Annette came with them, for the situation was then getting very dangerous in northern France, with skirmishes breaking out and risking the lives of the local people. She was about fifteen years old when she arrived in England."

"Very young to leave the rest of your family behind," said Julia.

"I'm not sure that there was any other family to leave. Anyway, Annette found work in a large house further north in Dorset, a live-in job helping care for the younger children. And you can probably guess what happened next."

"The elder son of the house made her pregnant? And didn't want to have anything to do with her afterwards?"

"Exactly! A very common story! Her sister agreed to take the child and bring him up with her own family near Bridport. But they had no room for Annette as well, nor could she find another job locally. So she travelled to London and sought another post there, and was taken on by the Brandons."

"So Frank Jepson is her son, and he may be able to speak some French if he was brought up by his aunt?"

"Yes. She didn't tell the Countess all this when she first worked for the family, of course, but when Annette was promoted to be her personal maid, they got to know each other much better, and little by little the story came out."

"Do you suspect that Annette is part of the smuggling ring?"

"No, probably not, but it might explain how Dominic got to know about it, and even perhaps how he met Patrick Jepson. My aunt wanted to know what the reason was for my interest, and I explained as much as I could without mentioning the possible connection with my cousin. She says that Annette is very honest, and very loyal to her own family and to the Brandons."

"So," said Julia, "there are two things missing now. A proven link between the smuggling ring and Frank Jepson, and something to show that Dominic was drawn into that business through Annette, presumably to make some money quickly."

"I spoke to my cousin Freddie before we came here. He is of the view that, if he can get Dominic in his cups, he might be able to get him to admit that he has been using Annette as a go-between."

"Yes, but the first point that I mentioned, about Frank Jepson, can only be done in Dorset. I should be able to persuade Aunt Lucy to send another letter to Mr. Hatton—he might be able to think of something."

Julia blushed as she said this, but her sisters calling them to come downstairs to join Freddie meant that Emily did not notice.

Before they left to return to the castle, Freddie told Julia that he would be travelling to town on the following day with his father, and hoped to have some conversation with his brother before the end of the week.

That evening, Julia brought Aunt Lucy up to date with the story, and she was delighted to assist.

"Do you know, Julia, I was really quite bored before you came with Emily to stay with me in Bath. And despite my having that painful ankle for a few days, my life has been so much more pleasant and interesting ever since. Of course I will write to Mr. Hatton. Do you know whether his father is still there with him in Dorset?"

"Well, there is something interesting, or perhaps amusing, that Papa told me yesterday."

"What was that?"

"Kit—I mean Mr. Hatton—told me at Morancourt that his

father was going to travel by stagecoach with his valet from Derbyshire to Bath, for he is very prudent with money. We had a laugh together about that. But Papa has told me that he had received a letter earlier this week from Mr. Douglas, saying exactly the opposite. Apparently Kit insisted that Mr. Douglas travel all the way from Derbyshire to Dorset in his own carriage, saying that he, Mr. Hatton, would be disgraced in the whole neighbourhood around Morancourt if his father arrived by the post."

"That surprises me, for Mr. Hatton did not seem to be someone who would care about that?"

"No," said Julia. "Exactly, I agree."

"When is Mr. Douglas expected to return home?"

"That was the main purpose of the letter, Papa said. Mr. Douglas was due to leave Morancourt about two days ago. I suppose that he might make a short stop in Bath, but he should be back at Norton Place by the end of this week. I know that my father is looking forward very much to seeing him."

Julia had assumed that Aunt Lucy would not stay very long at Banford Hall before returning home, for usually she and Mama found that a few days were enough in each other's company, but so far no mention had been made of a date for her aunt to leave for Bath. Julia suspected that she was not only waiting for a reply to her letter from Mr. Hatton, but also to see if any news came from Freddie in town.

Mama took Julia aside one morning and told her quietly that the local doctor would be making one of his regular visits to the house in an hour's time to examine Papa's condition.

Julia asked her mother whether she thought that Papa was getting worse. Her mother did not often show emotion, but Julia could see that tears came readily to her eyes as she replied, "I fear so, although I have said nothing to your sisters. The physician does not tell me very much."

The doctor came at the appointed time and went in to examine his patient. After a little while, he called Mama in to join him.

Aunt Lucy was in the drawing room and Sophie and Harriet were upstairs when Julia heard the noise of more carriage wheels on the gravel at the front of the house, and she went into the hall.

When the housekeeper opened the door, Harry Douglas was standing in the entrance, and Julia was surprised to see just behind him a tall white-haired gentleman, smartly dressed in city clothes and with a black bag in his hand.

"Mr. Douglas! How good to see you! It is so long since we met. Please come in, and your companion also."

"Thank you, Miss Maitland. I am equally delighted to see you. Can we please go into the dining room?"

Surprised, she did as he asked, for she would normally have taken the visitors into the drawing room and then gone to find her mother.

There Mr. Douglas continued, "This gentleman has been most kind in travelling with me in my carriage all the way from Bath. Is Mrs. Maitland at home?"

Julia looked doubtful. "She is in the dressing room with Papa, Mr. Douglas, where the local physician is carrying out one of his regular examinations of my father's condition."

"In that case, the timing of our visit is most opportune. Would you please ask Mrs. Maitland and the local doctor to join us here? It is very important."

Julia was surprised at this request, but did as she was asked.

Her mother was not at all happy with the interruption, but Julia eventually persuaded her to comply and to bring the physician with her.

When they entered the dining room together, Mr. Douglas said, "Mrs. Maitland, I do most sincerely apologise for not giving you any prior warning of my visit. However, I would like to introduce Sir William Knighton to you."

Mama looked blank, but the local physician exclaimed without hesitation, "Sir William, I am so honoured to meet you!"

Julia and her mother waited for an explanation as the doctor continued.

"How exceptionally fortunate, sir! Your name and your excellent reputation for treating problems of the heart are well known to my profession even in this very rural location. Mrs. Maitland, if your husband is to improve, this is the gentleman who can achieve it."

TWELVE

Sir William, Mama, and the doctor were soon closeted in the dressing room with Papa, and Julia found herself alone with Mr. Douglas in the dining room.

"I wish you to be assured, Miss Maitland, that none of the expenses for Sir William's consultation will fall upon your family."

Julia would have been inclined to argue this point, but something in his expression convinced her that that would be a total waste of time. Instead, she replied, "In that case, may I thank you from the bottom of my heart, for I have heard of Sir William's excellent professional reputation."

To her surprise, Mr. Douglas looked very embarrassed and, after hesitating, he said, "Miss Maitland, if you will promise not to tell anyone else? What I told you is not the full truth of the matter."

She indicated her agreement, although perplexed at his remark.

"It was Kit who was adamant that I should take my own coach all the way down to Bath, though he would not tell me why. Only at the end of my stay at Morancourt did he inform me that he had arranged for Sir William to be available to make the return journey north with me to Derbyshire, to visit your father.

Kit insists that I should take all the credit for the arrangements, but has refused to let me pay any of the expenses."

Julia had to smile to herself at his barely concealed indignation at his son's insistence.

"I do not like 'sailing under false colours' in this matter, but my only role has been to provide the transport for us back to Derbyshire, and then to return Sir William today to Derby, so that he can take the stagecoach south and get back to Windsor."

"Why does he want to go to Windsor, Mr. Douglas? I thought that his main consulting rooms were in Bath?"

"It is true that he practices from there, but I have been told that he is the chief physician-in-residence to His Majesty the King," said Mr. Douglas, this time with pride in his voice.

Julia was speechless at this information, for she had no idea of that connection. What would Mama say? Julia suspected that her mother's opinion of Harry Douglas was going to increase several hundredfold when she heard all this.

"I have a commission from K—I mean from Mr. Hatton— to pass on some information only to you in private, Miss Maitland. Is your aunt, Mrs. Harrison, still staying here with you? If so, would it be possible for both of you to visit Norton Place tomorrow?"

Before Julia could reply, she heard her aunt and her sisters calling for her in the hall, and she took Mr. Douglas from the dining room to be introduced to Aunt Lucy. She was clearly very intrigued to meet him, although unable with both Sophie and Harriet within earshot to acknowledge her previous acquaintance with his younger son as she might have wished.

Upon hearing of the invitation from Mr. Douglas, she immediately agreed to go with Julia to Norton Place on the following day, and the only problem was resisting the protestations from

Sophie and Harriet at the news that they were not to be included in the party. Mr. Douglas took their dissent in good part, and promised that they might visit him on another occasion.

Sir William did not emerge with Mama and the physician from the dressing room for some time but, when they did, it was easy to see from her expression that the news was much better than before.

On becoming aware of the eager audience waiting for them at the bottom of the stairs, Sir William said, in an avuncular style, "Well, ladies, Mrs. Maitland will tell you the details, but I am confident that Mr. Maitland's doctor can carry out my instructions, and that the results should be beneficial. Now, Mr. Douglas, we had best be on our way if I am to catch the stage south from Derby today."

Mama was indeed very gracious to Mr. Douglas as they left, as Julia had foreseen, and said as soon as the front door had closed, "My dear Lucy, it is such better news as far as Lewis is concerned. And Sir William has told me that he has strict instructions to render his bill for payment only to Mr. Douglas, who took all the trouble to arrange that consultation, and no charge at all is to fall upon us. That is so generous of him!"

Her eldest daughter then intervened. "Did you know, Mama, that Sir William is a personal physician to the king himself?"

There was a stunned silence, as Julia had anticipated, and then a hubbub of sound as everyone asked questions at once, and some minutes passed before order was restored. When Aunt Lucy told Mama of the invitation for Julia to visit Norton Place with her aunt the next day, Mama was all smiles and gracious agreement.

They travelled together in Aunt Lucy's chaise—much more comfortable than the last time I took this journey, thought

Julia—and on the way her aunt inquired what Julia thought the purpose of the visit might be.

"Did Mr. Douglas give any indication to you?"

"No, he didn't. There may be some news about the smugglers, although Mr. Hatton could have sent a letter to you about that."

"Will I like Norton Place, Julia?"

"Yes, I think so. I had expected it to be rather—how can I say—brash? But that was because I was prejudging the house through Mama's eyes, for she was determined to look down on Mr. Douglas as someone who 'bought his own furniture'—a self-made man."

Her aunt chuckled. "I doubt whether you will be having that problem with your mother in the future, after what happened yesterday!"

Julia laughed and agreed. With a pleasant and sympathetic companion beside her, the journey passed very quickly and the chaise was soon coming to a halt in front of Norton Place. Julia had forgotten to ask Mr. Douglas whether Jack would be at home, but there was no sign of him in the house as Mr. Douglas led the way to the drawing room.

Much to Julia's amusement, for the first half hour she was quite sidelined, as their host and her aunt soon proved to have many views in common, and conducted a wide-ranging conversation over various topics. It was only when the butler came in to ask if tea should be served that Harry Douglas turned to Julia and apologised for his lack of attention.

"Now, Miss Maitland, first of all I have a note to give to you from Kit. He asks that you should read it through first, and he told me that there were some parts that you could then pass on to us."

There was a real twinkle in his eye as he said this, and Julia suddenly wondered how much Kit had told his father about their relationship.

However, the letter was already in her hand, and she skimmed it quickly. The first half was very intriguing, and the last page so intimately heart-warming that her aunt and Mr. Douglas must be able to see her blushing.

"What is the news?" said Aunt Lucy, coming to her rescue.

"Well, Kit—Mr. Hatton—has spoken to Mr. Whitaker, his farm manager, about whether he had had any suspicions about the estate land or buildings being used for smuggling. Mr. Whitaker told him that he had come to think that might be the case, and that he had wondered if Mr. Jones, the husband of the housekeeper, knew more about it."

"Did you meet Mr. Whitaker or Mr. Jones?" Aunt Lucy asked Mr. Douglas.

"Yes, both of them, and they did not seem to me to be dishonest men. But perhaps I'm wrong?"

Julia continued, "Mr. Hatton goes on to say that when he asked Mr. Jones about 'free traders' operating on the estate, he confessed that when he came back many years ago from being a soldier in France, he had become involved in smuggling with Isaac Gulliver. But he said that he had finished with that when he was given charge of the farm at Morancourt by Mr. Henry Hatton."

"So he knows nothing of what is happening now?"

"No, he does. Indeed, he had already heard from Mr. Gulliver that we had been to visit the earthwork at Eggardon!"

Mr. Douglas looked puzzled, so Julia explained about her visit with Mr. Hatton to the hill fort, and the man whom they had met there claiming to be a priest.

"Apparently, Mr. Hatton says that Isaac Gulliver is a very

unusual smuggler. His men are kept constantly at work smuggling wine and other goods, mostly through the village of Burton Bradstock. Some wear Dorset smocks, as used by farm workers, and with their hair powdered like wigs, as a kind of livery to identify them. They are forbidden to offer any physical harm to the revenue men. It is his dislike of violence that led to his opposing another gang, which started operating in the area around Bridport about eighteen months ago."

Julia then remembered that Aunt Lucy knew nothing about Frank Jepson, and so explained briefly, without mentioning any connection with the Brandons, what was known about him.

Then she went on, "Aunt Lucy, there was something that I did not tell you when we were at Morancourt. A young man called Jem, who proved to be the brother of Martha, your personal maid, was brought into the kitchen there with an injury to his leg. Mrs. Jones, the housekeeper, did not know who he was, and he refused to acknowledge his sister. Martha asked me not to mention him or his injury to you."

"Why not? Did she suspect that he was up to no good?"

"Probably."

"Was that the same brother that she had told us about on the journey down to Dorset, who had been a miner near Radstock?"

"Yes, it was. Kit has since traced him after another conversation with Mr. Jones. Jem had been lodging in the village, and working with several other men for Frank Jepson with good pay, smuggling goods into Dorset on the coast near Bridport. When he injured his leg carrying a heavy load, Jepson threatened to break his arm, or worse, if he told anyone how the injury had happened."

"That Frank Jepson sounds to be a nasty piece of work," said Mr. Douglas.

"Yes, and he stopped paying Jem as soon as he hurt himself, because he was of no more use to the smuggling gang. Kit thought that it would be safest for Jem to go back to stay with his mother at Radstock as soon as possible, so that he was outside Frank Jepson's reach. Kit gave Jem some money to keep him going until his leg heals and he can get a job as a miner again near Radstock."

"So what is Kit doing now about the smuggling gang?" said his father.

"He has had a long discussion with his friend James Lindsay, who is close to being able to prove that the smuggling gang using the buildings at Morancourt is under the control of Frank Jepson. The revenue men have already found several other places on the estate where contraband goods are being hidden."

"What are those?" said Mr. Douglas.

"Apparently they found that someone had dug along the slope of the hill above one of the lynchets that we saw on our walk on the way to the old castle. Contraband had been hidden underground there, not long ago, before it was concealed by being covered with earth."

"And is Kit involved personally in the hunt for Frank Jepson?" said Aunt Lucy.

"No, Sir James has told him that would be unwise. Kit says only," she blushed, "that I should not worry about him."

Aunt Lucy smiled at her niece. "Mr. Douglas, I believe that you have another son living with you here?"

"Yes, ma'am, that is my elder son, Jack. But I have sent him to work at my mill in Leeds, to learn more about managing the business."

Julia was very surprised at this news, and her host, foreseeing her question, said, "It will be good for Jack to be busy elsewhere for a while. I have appointed a new manager for our farm here, with more up-to-date ideas. You will know about that, Miss Maitland, as you spoke to me before about the practices introduced at Holkham."

"Yes, sir," said Julia dutifully, but with a twinkle in her eye to match the smile from Harry Douglas.

"You are lucky, Mrs. Harrison, to have such a lively niece!"

"I know that, Mr. Douglas, but I have formed the opinion that your younger son is a very worthwhile young man as well."

Mr. Douglas looked very pleased at this remark, and again Julia wondered what Mr. Hatton had told him about her stay at Morancourt.

"That reminds me, Miss Maitland. Kit asked to give you something—I have tried to wrap it carefully for you, but I am not very neat-fingered at such things!"

Harry Douglas turned to a side table, picked up a small package, and gave it to her. Julia unwrapped it slowly and found herself looking at a book. It was *La Passerelle*.

"Oh no!" She could not stop the expression escaping her lips. "That belongs to Kit."

Aunt Lucy looked at her with concern, as did Harry Douglas, but before either of them could say anything, Julia smiled at them tearfully.

"It is just—oh, it is the most wonderful present that anyone could have given to me, but I really cannot accept it."

"Why not, Julia? What is it?" said her aunt.

"You will know, Aunt, if I tell you that this book is the real *La Passerelle*!"

Mr. Douglas still looked confused, but Aunt Lucy visibly relaxed at her recognition of the name.

"Mr. Douglas," she said, "perhaps Julia would like to go

and sit for a while to examine the book in your library. There is something that I wish to discuss with you."

Julia was inclined to rebel at this explicit instruction, but decided that it was best to do as she was asked. Fully fifteen minutes then passed before her host came to the door and asked her to rejoin them in the drawing room.

"Please take the book home with you, Miss Maitland. You can look after it for Kit until he is next back here at Norton Place. I have had a very useful conversation with Mrs. Harrison, and hope that she can come here again before she returns home to Bath."

On the way home in the carriage, Aunt Lucy said, with a half smile, "Am I the only person who thinks that Mr. Douglas might have been getting his elder son out of your way?"

Julia looked puzzled for a moment, then said slowly, "Do you mean that Harry Douglas has deliberately sent Jack away so that my mother, or even my father, can't pursue the idea of his being a suitor for me?"

"Or perhaps Kit Hatton asked him to consider the matter. It would certainly be a good idea from his point of view?"

Julia blushed, considered, and then replied, "I certainly was very surprised to hear that Jack had been sent to Leeds, for Mr. Douglas once told me that his late wife did not wish either of their sons to work in trade."

"Perhaps Mr. Douglas has decided that Jack is better suited to that than any other occupation. For the moment, I suggest that we do not tell your mama that Jack is no longer living at Norton Place."

"Aunt Lucy, I do believe that you have missed your true vocation as a matchmaker!"

"No, my dear, I just wish you to be happy, and I have been receiving some good advice this afternoon!"

Julia's cheerful frame of mind on returning to Banford Hall did not last long, for Emily had called in their absence, to say Julia was invited to visit there on the following day.

"On my own?" said Julia, dismayed at the thought of another visit.

"No," said Mama in a disapproving tone. "Emily has told us that her aunt and uncle insist that your Aunt Lucy should accompany you on this occasion."

Her elder daughter stared at her in amazement.

"But—"

"Yes, I know, the Earl and Countess have never met Lucy, but I did not feel that I could insist that I should go with you instead. I suppose that I am not grand enough for them!"

And with that, her mother swept out of the room, leaving Julia and her aunt looking at Harriet, who had been standing quietly by during this conversation.

"Did Emily say anything else to you that she did not tell Mama?"

"Only one brief message for you, Julia. She said to tell you that the Jepson link had been established. She told me that you would understand what that meant."

Aunt Lucy seemed about to ask a question, but then said, "One day, Julia, you must tell me the whole story, not just part of it." And with that, she left the room, leaving the two sisters together.

"I suppose that you can't tell me, either?" said her younger sister.

"For the moment, no, but I will one day, I promise. It must be good news, or I hope it is, for, if not, I might be about to receive an unwelcome marriage proposal that I would find very difficult to refuse."

During the drive to Cressborough Castle the next day, Julia could sense that her aunt was bursting with curiosity about the relevance of the Jepson connection and Emily Brandon. But instead she remarked on how fine they both looked, wearing their most stylish dresses at Mama's insistence.

"Do you think, dear aunt, that one should dress in one's best finery just because one is to visit an earl and countess?"

Aunt Lucy looked at her for a moment, thinking how well the blue dress fitted her slim figure and suited her colouring.

"No, my dear. But you have told me that they have both always been very pleasant to you, so perhaps we would have worn the same clothes even if your ambitious mama had not intervened."

Aunt Lucy was very taken with the imposing entrance to the castle, though she said quietly to her niece that she was beginning to sound too much like her sister, Olivia. They were received with the usual formalities, and found Emily with her uncle and aunt in the drawing room.

Julia introduced her aunt, and the Earl said, "You are most welcome, Mrs. Harrison. We are very grateful for your kindness to Emily in Bath a few weeks ago."

"It was a pleasure," she replied, smiling at Emily as she took a seat opposite her hosts.

The Countess did not waste any time in coming to the point.

"Julia, first of all, we owe you a most sincere apology. As you know, we had been encouraging you to believe that Dominic would be willing to marry you—an alliance that both the Earl and I favoured, as we had explained to you previously. Instead, we have discovered this week that Dominic was married a few days ago in London without our consent—to a young woman whose past history has been far from blameless, and who will not be a welcome addition to our family."

Julia glanced at Emily before the Countess continued.

"Emily has told me that you know that Dominic had been seeing this young woman in London, contrary to our express instructions and wishes. We have also discovered from Freddie that Dominic had been getting deeper and deeper into debt."

Julia nodded, as some sort of acknowledgement was apparently expected.

"Mrs. Harrison, we asked you to escort Julia today rather than her mother because Emily has told us that we can rely entirely on your discretion. You can understand that we are not anxious for all the details of this matter to get around society here in Derbyshire."

"I understand, Lady Brandon," said Aunt Lucy.

"But Julia, we wish to ask you something further. Emily has told us that Dominic may have got into seriously bad company. That he may, unbelievable as it seems, have taken it upon himself, together with a London acquaintance, Mr. Jepson, to sell contraband goods to his society friends, to make money to pay his gambling debts. Is there any truth in that, to your knowledge?"

Julia took a deep breath and glanced quickly at her aunt, who was observing her with a certain amount of relish.

"My lord, Emily may have told you that Mr. Hatton was our host in Dorset. Various events occurred whilst I was staying there with Mrs. Harrison that indicated that unauthorised activities might be taking place in the buildings at Morancourt. I have heard since from Mr. Hatton through—through a friend—that a close relative of Mr. Jepson was involved in smuggling various valuable goods from France despite the blockade in the English Channel."

Julia had to feel sorry for the Earl and Countess, who looked so stricken at this confirmation of the news they had dreaded.

The Earl explained, "Emily has found out that Dominic was drawn into this illegal trade by one of our own employees, who has a connection with this fellow Jepson. We are both leaving for town tomorrow, to bring Dominic and his—his new bride—back to Cressborough to make their home here, since he clearly cannot be trusted to live sensibly in London."

"I am so sorry," said Julia. "This must all be most upsetting for you both. But please do not concern yourselves about me. There was no formal engagement, and I had been keeping an open mind about the suggestion."

Her aunt intervened. "My sister, Mrs. Maitland, had, as you know, been very happy at the possibility of a marriage to your heir, but I am sure that Julia and I can inform her of the situation without revealing anything that you might prefer not to be disclosed."

Emily had been sitting listening to this conversation, but now could not contain herself any longer.

"Well, I think it is all for the better, for Julia could find herself someone far more suitable than my silly cousin. Freddie would never have been so stupid!"

"Emily," Julia said swiftly, "you are being very loyal to me, but it is so easy for young gentlemen with plenty of money to be led astray in London."

Both Julia and Aunt Lucy noticed that the Earl looked rather uncomfortable at this remark, and could guess the reason.

"Once Dominic is here at home away from bad influences, I'm sure he will settle down, for he is not an unkind person. Indeed, he was very pleasant and very fair in discussing an alliance with me. Although I only saw Christina once in the distance, when I went to the Vauxhall Gardens with Emily and Freddie, she looked to be a most beautiful girl, and may have a very pleasant personality for all we know."

"You are most charitable, my dear," said the Countess, "and I hope that Dominic will realise in time how much he has lost by his thoughtless behaviour."

"Can I suggest," said Aunt Lucy," that it would be sensible, once the young couple has settled here, if Julia is seen in their company, to confirm that there is no ill feeling?"

"Of course," said her host, "that is an excellent idea, and Julia will always be welcome here in any case, as a friend of us all."

It was, Julia reflected on the return journey, one of the most extraordinary visits she had ever made. Aunt Lucy insisted on knowing all the details about the smuggling ring that she had not already heard, and they discussed how to present the news to Mama and Papa when they got back to Banford Hall.

Mama took the news that Dominic Brandon preferred a young woman from London to her own daughter very badly. She was reluctant to believe that the Earl and Countess had known little about the situation, and would have liked to blame Julia, although Aunt Lucy was having none of that.

Papa was more sanguine, despite saying nothing to Mama, since he knew very well that Julia would be quite delighted at the news.

Mama proved, however, to be nothing but adaptable. Over the next few days, Mama was often in Papa's room, and Julia was sure that they were discussing her future prospects.

Despite the hope that Papa's health would improve with Sir William Knighton's advice, Mama still seemed determined that Julia's marriage should not be delayed very much longer. Her younger sisters tried to cheer her by making various outlandish suggestions as to possible suitors living in the county, but Julia could not joke about the matter anymore. She could not know what influence Papa was having on Mama's social ambitions for her daughter, so it was with considerable surprise that Julia heard her mother one morning telling Papa that "Julia should make a visit to Norton Place to see Jack Douglas, my dear."

Julia demurred strongly at this, but Mama eventually persuaded Papa to write a note to Harry Douglas, asking if he would like to bring his son over to Banford Hall instead, as Papa was not yet strong enough to make the journey to visit his friend.

Julia quite expected the reply to this suggestion to be negative, as she believed that Jack Douglas was still in Leeds. She was therefore surprised and very unhappy that the message came back that Mr. Douglas would be delighted to visit Banford Hall in a few days' time.

Harry Douglas arrived at the appointed time, but Jack was not with him. After the usual pleasantries, Mr. Douglas told Mama firmly that he wished to speak to Mr. Maitland in private.

Mama took him up to Papa's dressing room and came back almost purring with satisfaction, saying to her daughters, "I expect that Mr. Douglas wishes to discuss a financial settlement with your father."

"I don't see why he would," said Harriet firmly, "since that should surely wait until Julia has said that she will agree to marry Jack Douglas."

"Well, I think that Jack is a perfectly good catch. I liked him well enough," said Sophie.

Julia said nothing, misery being piled upon misery. Her only hope seemed to be that Papa would not agree without consulting her first.

After about an hour, Mr. Douglas came down the stairs and into the drawing room, and spoke much more firmly than was his habit to Mama.

"I understand that you would favour my son marrying your eldest daughter, Mrs. Maitland?"

Mama looked rather taken aback by his blunt way of speaking, but replied, "Why yes, sir, of course, if Mr. Maitland is agreeable."

No mention of what I might want! thought Julia.

"Very well. I am leaving now, and Lewis—Mr. Maitland— wishes to speak to Miss Maitland in private. Good day, ma'am, ladies."

He had hardly left the house than her mother was chivvying Julia to go and see her father. Aunt Lucy tried to protest, for she could see how angry her eldest niece was feeling, but Mama as usual brooked no opposition.

Julia walked slowly up the stairs, went into the dressing room, and shut the door. To her surprise, her father was looking very cheerful and sounded more decisive than usual.

"Now, Julia, I want you to do exactly as I tell you. Harry Douglas has invited Aunt Lucy to take you to Norton Place for a light luncheon tomorrow. Your mother would have liked to go with you, but I have not agreed to that."

"What is the purpose of the visit?" said Julia resentfully.

"To consider whether you would accept the option that he is offering to you."

"I do not need to go to Norton Place to tell you that. You really mean the option that Mama favours, and with the biggest financial settlement attached!"

"I suggest you wait and see what the offer may be. It could be trying out your Norfolk theories on his farm, perhaps?"

"I don't feel like joking," she replied.

"No, maybe not. When you return, we can have another private talk together if you wish."

And Papa would tell her no more than that. Julia, not often given to total despair, spent the rest of the day in deepest gloom. She found it very difficult to believe that her father would be happy about an alliance with Jack Douglas, but what other options were there, and what else could he mean?

Before they left the following morning, Julia insisted in wrapping up *La Passerelle* and taking the package with her, for she was determined to return it to Mr. Douglas, whatever he or her aunt might say.

The journey was made in Aunt Lucy's comfortable chaise and, as soon as Banford Hall was left behind, her aunt turned to Julia.

"My dear, I cannot believe that your father would have agreed to any alliance with Jack Douglas without your consent."

"Then why would Harry Douglas have said what he did to my mother?"

Aunt Lucy opened her mouth to reply, then she paused and looked at Julia and shut it again without any words coming out. This was so unlike her aunt that Julia fixed her with a determined stare and said, "What were you going to say?"

"What I was going to say was that you should consider what Harry Douglas did not mention yesterday."

"What was that?" Julia said resentfully.

"You must tell me, my dear, not I you."

Julia was already so upset that this remark put her into a really bad temper and she turned her face away to look fixedly out of the carriage window, and she refused to say anything for the rest of the journey. If she had glanced at her aunt, she would have been even more infuriated to see that Aunt Lucy was smiling to herself.

In his usual jovial way, Harry Douglas was waiting to welcome them at Norton Place by the bottom of the steps leading to the front door. Julia had intended to thrust the package containing *La Passerelle* into his hands as soon as she arrived, but her aunt's firm grasp of her arm prevented that. Julia found herself inside the house and walking beside Mr. Douglas along the corridor to the salon without having any option in the matter.

Once they were there, her host said to Aunt Lucy, "Have you said anything to Miss Maitland since yesterday?"

"No, sir," said her aunt.

Julia looked from the one to the other, mystified.

"You will have heard your mother, Mrs. Maitland, say that she would favour my son marrying her eldest daughter, if your father agreed? I imagine that you were not happy about that?"

She stared at him, then replied, "No sir, I was not—no one seems to think of consulting me about my own future! I wish to return *La Passerelle* to you now."

"Indeed. Now, please do as I ask. Take that package into the library, and leave it there if you wish. And when you are ready, come back and join us in the salon here."

He spoke calmly, and Julia's wrath was changing now to a dull ache of sadness, and she did not move.

"Julia," said Aunt Lucy, "please do as Mr. Douglas requests."

Julia glared at her and at last turned on her heel and walked along the corridor and into the library. She went across the room to the table by the window where she had seen the Book of Hours on her first visit to the house, and put the package down. She looked down and let her hand rest on the book for several moments, remembering that day. She raised her head and was about to turn to leave the room when she jumped in alarm, for there, reflected in the glass of the window, was a tall figure standing in the shadows beside the door, watching her. It was only when she turned to face him that he stepped forward into the light and she realised who it was.

He looked at her gravely. "My father tells me that you are very unlikely to want to marry his son, Miss Maitland. Does that apply to me, or are you willing to make an exception for a gentleman who, as you know, may never be able to waltz very well?"

Julia was at a loss for words. It had been such an emotional few hours since Mr. Douglas had visited Banford Hall to see her father, filled with sadness and fear for the future.

Kit Hatton walked slowly across the library towards her, then stopped just beyond touching distance and said, "I understand that Mr. Maitland and your mother are happy with the proposition that my father put to them yesterday, that you should marry me."

It was only then that Julia realised what Aunt Lucy had meant in the carriage. Harry Douglas had asked Mama if she would favour his son marrying her eldest daughter. But he had not said which son.

"Come, my darling," said Kit. "Everything really is all well for us both now." And he opened his arms to her as she wept tears of joy and relief. She had dreamt so many times of kissing Kit Hatton, but the reality surpassed what she had hoped for, and needed, and wanted.

Eventually they turned their attention to more practical matters. Kit told Julia how Aunt Lucy and Harry Douglas had collaborated together to pass on the news about Dominic Brandon's marriage, and Kit had set off immediately from Dorset to travel to Norton Place.

"About ten days ago, James Lindsay confronted his cousin Patrick about the connection with Dominic Brandon, and Patrick revealed many details about the distribution network for contraband that Dominic had been organising. Frank Jepson was caught by the revenue men a few days later as he landed with a large cargo of contraband at the bay near Morancourt. I wrote to your aunt, and she passed that information on to Emily Brandon, who told the earl and countess."

It was quite half an hour later when there was a firm cough in the doorway, and they both turned around to see Harry Douglas and Aunt Lucy standing side by side, regarding them with expressions of amusement and affection.

"Well, my dear," said her aunt, "are you still going to return *La Passerelle* to Mr. Douglas?"

"No, Aunt," said Julia meekly, "for Kit has told me that the book belongs to both of us from now on."

THE HISTORY
BEHIND
THE STORY

HISTORICAL FICTION
· ·

The term "historical fiction" is usually applied to a novel set in any period between the Dark Ages (before Christ) and the years immediately following the Second World War. The Historical Novel Society was founded in England in 1997, at a time when historical fiction was rather less popular than it is now, by a group of enthusiasts who volunteered to review novels being published on historical subjects.

As a keen reader of historical novels, I joined the Society in its early days, and it has continued to prosper with more and more readers, authors, publishers, and agents from the UK, and more recently from the US, becoming members. Over 100 volunteers now review about 800 books that have been published in the English language each year for the Society. HarperCollins authors like Tasha Alexander, Suzannah Dunn, Nicole Galland, and Robin Maxwell have all pleased readers with their novels about particular times in history.

REGENCY ROMANCES

Although I enjoy reading novels set in all different periods of history, I seem to return most frequently to those often described as Regency Romances, which are set in the early 1800s, a time originally immortalised by the English author Jane Austen, whose six novels remain as popular now as they were in the century when they were written. She surely would have been amazed by the "Jane Austen industry" which has prospered during the past few decades through books, TV series, and films, and in particular the enduring enthusiasm of readers for her most enigmatic hero. My novel *Darcy's Story* was written following the considerable success of the BBC TV series based on her best-loved book *Pride and Prejudice*. More recently, *Cassandra & Jane*, by Jill Pitkeathley, has delighted Jane Austen's fans.

At its simplest, a Regency Romance takes place in a "gilded cage," where a handsome hero and an attractive heroine move through grand stately homes to their destiny, apparently unaffected by the realities of everyday life.

But to me, the Regency period in England was more interesting than that. Sufficiently remote from the present day to be intriguing, and yet recent enough for there to be numerous written records of the changing patterns of life at that time, one can see the beginnings of what came to be known as the industrial revolution, the introduction of more sophisticated financial systems and the beginnings of a more emancipated life for educated women, all set against the backdrop of the war with Napoléon in the early years of the nineteenth century.

So the author of a Regency Romance has a choice. One is

to take the simple route in developing the story within a "gilded cage," and there are very many successful examples of that approach. The other option, and my preference, is to set the novel in a more realistic context, leading the reader through the way the world is changing around the characters as they approach their destiny.

The interaction between the different personalities in a family holds a particular interest for me. In my novel, the middle daughter, Sophie Maitland, took after her mother, Olivia, in being determined and irrepressible, running at everything in life at full-tilt, and could be very thoughtless. Her elder sister, Julia, also inherited her mother's determination, but otherwise was a much calmer person, like her father, as well as being sympathetic and practical. The ideal "partners in life" for each of the sisters are therefore very different, and their stories are likely to develop accordingly. Where a personality is less clear-cut, as with the youngest sister, Harriet Maitland, there may appear to be more options, although most of her character would already have been formed when she was much younger.

LIFE IN THE EARLY 1800s

During the Regency period, the divisions between social classes began to ease, although the life of titled families and the gentry was still controlled by rigid formalities. Improved methods of cultivation, husbandry, and the use of simple machinery were pioneered by wealthy farmers such as Thomas Coke of Norfolk, which led to higher crop yields, healthier animals, and increased incomes for the landed gentry. The extra food produced also allowed for a significant growth in the country's population.

The rise in the size of the population in England by the early 1800s provided not only more young men and women to work in the new factories and mills, especially in the north of England, but also a greater number of people available to be servants in the wealthier households. Although they were sometimes abused by their employers, recent research confirms that servants working in stately homes were likely to live much longer than if they had been employed in factories or remained in a farming job in the countryside.

In the grandest families, such as the Brandons in my novel, the children might well have much closer emotional ties with the servants who looked after them than they did with their parents, who they might have seen very rarely. That seems to have been the situation for Dominic Brandon and Annette Labonne, who had been a nurse to the two sons of the Earl and Countess of Cressborough.

Indeed, servants often knew a great deal about what was happening in the privacy of the household. In my novel, Julia Maitland's widowed aunt, Mrs. Lucy Harrison, sends her maid Martha away when they travel back to Julia's home in

Derbyshire, so that she cannot tell Julia's family anything about what happened during their stay in Dorset with Mr. Hatton.

It is not difficult to see why a wealthy young man like Dominic Brandon, who might not know his parents very well, would decide that he did not want to live at home in the country with them. He preferred to waste away his time in London with his friends, trying to live on his allowance from the Earl whilst gambling, drinking, and pursuing young women of the commoner sort, especially since that was the example that had been set by his father.

However, not everyone was like Kit Douglas in my book or Jane Austen's brother Edward in real life, hoping to inherit the house and estate of a wealthy and childless relative. Many young gentlemen served in the army or navy, at least for a few years. The elder son of a landed family could expect to inherit the estate, but his younger brothers might need to continue to remain in the army or navy or elsewhere in the longer term. If they did not choose a military or naval life, the Church, or, to a lesser extent, the law were amongst the few respectable options for employment open to them. But, however socially acceptable an occupation, a young man serving in the army or Royal Navy risked injury during the war with Napoléon, as was the case with Kit Douglas, or at worst might be killed, as happened to Julia Maitland's elder brother, David, and Sir James Lindsay, the father of Kit's friend.

The choices available to young ladies of quality were much more limited. If they were wealthy with a handsome dowry or the sole heiress to a great estate, they were not likely to lack suitors keen to marry them. But when, as in the case of the Maitland sisters, the family estate was likely to pass to a distant relation on the death of a father or brother, the situation could be much more precarious. A very attractive young woman, such as Jane or

Elizabeth Bennet in *Pride and Prejudice*, might be sought-after because of her looks, but the lack of a respectable dowry could mean that the only viable options for a young girl might be to become a dependant helping the family in the home of a wealthy relation, or to go and work as a governess to the children of another family.

Thus Olivia Maitland in my novel was driven not only by her social ambitions for her eldest daughter to marry into a titled family but also by her concern for what the alternative might be for Julia's future. In some ways being a wealthy but childless widow, like Julia's Aunt Lucy (or the late Mrs. Hatton, godmother to Kit Douglas in my book), was the best situation of all, putting her in control of her own money and property, and free to do as she liked with both.

Inventions such as the spinning mule and power loom and the use of water wheels to drive machinery led to craft industries, such as weaving, being transferred from the rural homes into mills in both rural and urban locations. Other technical inventions aided the development of mining and other industrial enterprises, but their introduction sometimes led to riots and loss of life if the installation of even one machine deprived several men of their jobs.

However, many businessmen and entrepreneurs, like Harry Douglas in this story, left their old lives behind to become wealthy and prosperous, often married well, and were eventually able to buy social respectability by purchasing a handsome country house. Although some prejudice remained against "self-made men," it often took only a couple of generations for the modest origins of a gentleman to be forgotten and for his descendants' owning a rural estate to be fully accepted amongst the landed gentry.

By the early 1800s, many parents had become more willing

to take the personal preferences of their children into account when deciding whom they should marry. However, the cachet of a title could still be very persuasive, and Julia Maitland's mother was not unusual in being prepared to ignore the personal failings of Dominic Brandon because he was the heir to a great estate, so that her eldest daughter could have the certain prospect of becoming a countess if she married him.

But behaviour that might be seen as high spirits in well-born young gentleman was completely unacceptable in their sisters, who were expected to behave with proper decorum if they were to "marry well." Enlightened parents encouraged their daughters to learn to read and write, either at home or by sending them to school, as well as learning household management and "genteel" pursuits such as drawing, embroidery, or playing the piano. Books, in particular literary novels, became more readily available, whether from a lending library or for sale to those who could afford to buy them.

Well-intentioned family members, such as Julia Maitland's Aunt Lucy, could offer a valuable service by introducing young ladies to "the season" in London or a spa town. Fashionable places such as Bath and Brighton offered seasonal entertainments to rival those in London, including concerts as well as plays performed in the newly built theatres. There were other pastimes, such as visiting pleasure gardens, open to young people. The first balloon flights took place before the turn of the previous century and, by the early 1800s, were a not uncommon feature in some English towns and cities. More sophisticated carriages were developed, such as the curricle (the "racing car" of the day) and were driven by men of quality in competition with their friends, or to impress the young ladies. But their sisters usually had to be content with the occasional opportunity to take the reins of a curricle, if at all, in the privacy of the family's estate.

Dances and other social events in places such as Bath were opportunities for young ladies of marriageable age to meet a much larger number of eligible young men than was possible in a rural area with few neighbours and at some distance from a town of any size. Initially, dancing was still a very formal affair, and there was always a chaperone for a young woman in a public ballroom. The introduction of the waltz in 1815, with the couple dancing together in a semi-embrace, was revolutionary because it allowed an intimacy between the sexes that was very different from the existing more formal dances such as the cotillion or the quadrille, which were based on a set of eight or more participants.

OTHER ASPECTS OF LIFE IN THE 1800s
· · · · · · · · · ·

A wider choice of fabrics like silk and fine wines and other luxury goods became available at this time but, during the Napoleonic blockade, could only be obtained by smuggling across the English Channel from France and Spain, with the associated high costs. The transport of goods within the country was being revolutionised by the digging of canals to transport products from mills and factories to the major towns and cities, but personal travel by coach or on horseback was still a slow and uncomfortable business on badly made roads.

The progress of the economy at home could be very uneven. Although many new banks were founded by the gentry and businessmen during the Regency period to invest in land and new technical innovations, a bad harvest or a renewal of the conflict with Napoléon could lead to "a run" on a bank, which could bankrupt its investors, or at best mean that honourable gentleman such as Julia's father Lewis Maitland saw their incomes severely affected. In that situation, having friends with money or connections, like Harry Douglas or the Earl of Cressborough in my story, could make all the difference until easier times came along.

Another unpredictable aspect of life in the early 1800s was health and survival. Many women, like four of Jane Austen's own sisters-in-law, died early in childbirth because of the limitations of medical knowledge at the time. Few other health problems were fully understood. A fashionable doctor based in London or one of the spa towns could make a very good living, especially if they obtained a royal patron like Sir William Knighton, but Julia Maitland and her family in my novel had good cause to be fearful about her father's heart condition. Many events in history would have had a very different outcome if modern medical knowledge had been available.

FURTHER READING

•••••••••••••••••••

For further study on this period, I recommend the following.

BOOKS ABOUT ASPECTS OF LIFE IN THE REGENCY PERIOD

Life in the English Country House, by Mark Girouard (Yale University Press, 1978)

Flunkeys and Scullions: Life Below Stairs in Georgian England, by Pamela Horn, (Sutton Publishing, 2004)

Georgette Heyer's Regency World, by Jennifer Kloester (William Heinemann, 2005)

English Society in the Eighteenth Century, by Roy Porter (Penguin Books, 1982)

The Vital Century: England's Developing Economy, 1714–1815, by John Rule (Longman, 1992)

Jane Austen in Context, edited by Janet Todd (Cambridge University Press, 2005)

BOOKS ABOUT HISTORICAL EVENTS AFFECTING DORSET

Christian Slaves, Muslim Masters: White Slavery in the Mediterranean, the Barbary Coast, and Italy, 1500–1800, by Robert C. Davis (Palgrave Macmillan, 2003)

Smuggling in Hampshire and Dorset, 1700–1850, by Geoffrey Morley (Countryside Books, 1983)

One of the Few Regency Novels to Mention Contemporary Technical Inventions

Frederica, by Georgette Heyer (Arrow Books, 1965)

Two Books About Jane Austen

Jane Austen's England, by Maggie Lane (Robert Hale Limited, 1995)
Jane Austen: A Life, by Claire Tomalin (Penguin Books, 2000)

The lighter side of HISTORY

* Look for this seal on select historical fiction titles from Harper. Books bearing it contain special bonus materials, including timelines, interviews with the author, and insights into the real-life events that inspired the book, as well as recommendations for further reading.

AND ONLY TO DECEIVE:
A Novel of Suspense
by Tasha Alexander
978-0-06-114844-6 (paperback)
Discover the dangerous secrets kept by the strait-laced English of the Victorian era.

ANNETTE VALLON:
A Novel of the French Revolution
by James Tipton
978-0-06-082222-4 (paperback)
For fans of Tracy Chevalier and Sarah Dunant comes this vibrant, alluring debut novel of a compelling, independent woman who would inspire one of the world's greatest poets and survive a nation's bloody transformation.

BOUND: A Novel
by Sally Gunning
978-0-06-124026-3 (paperback)
An indentured servant finds herself bound by law, society, and her own heart in colonial Cape Cod.

THE CANTERBURY PAPERS: A Novel
by Judith Healey
978-0-06-077332-8 (paperback)
Follow Princess Alais on a secret mission as she unlocks a long-held and dangerous secret.

CASSANDRA & JANE: A Jane Austen Novel
by Jill Pitkeathley
978-0-06-144639-9 (paperback)
The relationship between Jane Austen and her sister—explored through the letters that might have been.

CROSSED: A Tale of the Fourth Crusade
by Nicole Galland
978-0-06-084180-5 (paperback)
Under the banner of the Crusades, a pious knight and a British
vagabond attempt a daring rescue.

DARCY'S STORY
by Janet Aylmer
978-0-06-114870-5 (paperback)
Read Mr. Darcy's side of the story—*Pride
and Prejudice* from a new perspective.

A FATAL WALTZ: A Novel of Suspense
by Tasha Alexander
978-0-06-117423-0 (paperback)
Caught in a murder mystery, Emily must do
the unthinkable to save her fiancé: bargain with
her ultimate nemesis, the Countess von Lange.

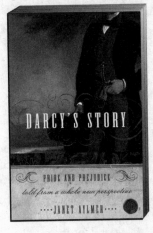

THE FIREMASTER'S MISTRESS: A Novel
by Christie Dickason
978-0-06-156826-8 (paperback)
Estranged lovers Francis and Kate rekindle their romance in the midst
of Guy Fawkes's plot to blow up Parliament.

THE FOOL'S TALE: A Novel
by Nicole Galland
978-0-06-072151-0 (paperback)
Travel back to Wales, 1198, a time of treachery, political unrest . . .
and passion.

JULIA AND THE MASTER OF MORANCOURT: A Novel
by Janet Aylmer
978-0-06-167295-8 (paperback)
Amidst family tragedy, Julia travels all over England, desperate to marry
the man she loves instead of the arranged suitor preferred by her mother.

KEPT: A Novel
by D. J. Tayler
978-0-06-114609-1 (paperback)
A gorgeously intricate, dazzling reinvention of
Victorian life and passions that is also a riveting
investigation into some of the darkest, most secret
chambers of the human heart.

PILATE'S WIFE: A Novel of the Roman Empire
by Antoinette May
978-0-06-112866-0 (paperback)
Claudia foresaw the Romans' persecution of Christians, but even she could not stop the crucifixion.

A POISONED SEASON: A Novel of Suspense
by Tasha Alexander
978-0-06-117421-6 (paperback)
As a cat-burglar torments Victorian London, a mysterious gentleman fascinates high society.

PORTRAIT OF AN UNKNOWN WOMAN: A Novel
by Vanora Bennett
978-0-06-125256-3 (paperback)
Meg, adopted daughter of Sir Thomas More, narrates the tale of a famous Holbein painting and the secrets it holds.

THE QUEEN OF SUBTLETIES: A Novel of Anne Boleyn
by Suzannah Dunn
978-0-06-059158-8 (paperback)
Untangle the web of fate surrounding Anne Boleyn in a tale narrated by the King's Confectioner.

THE QUEEN'S SORROW:
A Novel of Mary Tudor
by Suzannah Dunn
978-0-06-170427-7 (paperback)
Queen of England Mary Tudor's reign is brought low by abused power and a forbidden love.

REBECCA:
The Classic Tale of Romantic Suspense
by Daphne Du Maurier
978-0-380-73040-7 (paperback)
Follow the second Mrs. Maxim de Winter down the lonely drive to Manderley, where Rebecca once ruled.

REBECCA'S TALE: A Novel
by Sally Beauman
978-0-06-117467-4 (paperback)
Unlock the dark secrets and old worlds of Rebecca de Winter's life with investigator Colonel Julyan.

REVENGE OF THE ROSE: A Novel
by Nicole Galland
978-0-06-084179-9 (paperback)
In the court of the Holy Roman Emperor, not even a knight is safe from gossip, schemes, and secrets.

THE SIXTH WIFE: A Novel of Katherine Parr
by Suzannah Dunn
978-0-06-143156-2 (paperback)
Kate Parr survived four years of marriage to King Henry VIII, but a new love may undo a lifetime of caution.

TO THE TOWER BORN: A Novel of the Lost Princes
by Robin Maxwell
978-0-06-058052-0 (paperback)
Join Nell Caxton in the search for the lost heirs to the throne of Tudor England.

VIVALDI'S VIRGINS: A Novel
by Barbara Quick
978-0-06-089053-7 (paperback)
Abandoned as an infant, fourteen-year-old Anna Maria dal Violin is one of the elite musicians living in the foundling home where the "Red Priest," Antonio Vivaldi, is maestro and composer.

THE WIDOW'S WAR: A Novel
by Sally Gunning
978-0-06-079158-2 (paperback)
Tread the shores of colonial Cape Cod with a lonely whaler's widow as she tries to build a new life.

THE WILD IRISH:
A Novel of Elizabeth I & the Pirate O'Malley
by Robin Maxwell
978-0-06-009143-9 (paperback)
Hoist a sail with the Irish pirate and clan chief Grace O'Malley.

Available wherever books are sold, or call 1-800-331-3761 to order.